HINNOM MAGAZINE

October 2017

ISSUE 003

Edited by C.P. Dunphey

Publisher: Gehenna & Hinnom Books

Editor: C.P. Dunphey

Cover Art By: Travis Holmes

ISBN-10: 0-9972803-5-2

ISBN-13: 978-0-9972803-5-7

Printed in the United States of America.

First Edition.

Gehenna & Hinnom Books

Table of Contents:

HAPPY ALL HALLOWS' EVE
Introduction by C.P. Dunphey

Welcome to Gehenna & Hinnom.

Halloween is always a special time for us horror hounds and ghoulish fiends. Whether you fancy the darker side of various forms of entertainment or you simply enjoy celebrating the macabre, there is always excitement for fans of horror around this time of year.

While *Hinnom Magazine* specializes in many genres, our greatest passions continue to fall back into the realms of horror. There is something about a genre, defined by a human emotion, that piques the interest of so many people. One of the oldest genres that exists, horror perhaps finds itself timeless due to the presence of it in reality and our everyday lives.

Writing horror offers people the chance to express these dark experiences in a form of entertainment, which for many can be gratifying and even therapeutic. Why do we humans enjoy dangerous activities, like roller coasters and base jumping? Why do we pay to watch pugilism for sheer entertainment? Why are so many people thrill seekers?

Perhaps it is an ancient primordial instinct to show dominance or perseverance, survivability. We like to think it is because in our fears, and in the things that horrify us, we find the means to conquer. If that is the case, and Halloween is a time for us to face that which scares us, then we'd like to think Hallows' Eve is one of the best, if not most important holidays to exist.

In this magazine, you will find seven stories, selected over hundreds of others during our most abundant submissions process yet. We hope you will find these stories frightening, and that this Halloween, you will discover ways to conquer your own fears as well.

QUESTIONS FROM THE VOID:

An Interview with Dark Fiction author Philip Fracassi

(Originally published in The Gehenna Post)

Greetings from the Ethereal Plane,

To conclude our review series of Philip Fracassi's recent work, we present to you an interview with the dark fiction author. Following the success of his collection, *Behold the Void,* and our reviews of *Fragile Dreams, Sacculina,* and the aforementioned debut collection, it was exciting to delve into the mind of an author with such immense talent. We are beyond thrilled to share this interview with you, our readers, and hope that the fellow writers out there reading this article can garner some helpful information from Fracassi. Huge thanks go to Philip for agreeing to this venture and we cannot wait to put the interview into print with this month's edition of *Hinnom Magazine.*

Alas, let the interview begin!

CP: With the release of *Behold the Void,* the attention you've received from audiences along with the responses from critics and authors alike have all been well-deserved. You have been writing for a while now, between film scripts, short stories, chapbooks, and novellas. What does it mean to you, as a writer, to have a debut collection receive such praise?

PF: I don't know if writers have the ability to ever feel truly satisfied. For me, at least, my brain works like a demonic Stairmaster. The second I feel I've achieved something, I immediately click to the next tier of accomplishment and burn to achieve that higher step. When I published my chapbook (MOTHER, 2015), I was happy for about ten minutes, then started thinking about what to do next. Same with the collection. The minute it came out I immediately thought, "Okay, now what? What's the next step to reach for?" After the *New York Times* piece hit, people were saying stuff like, "Hey, you've made it!" But my attitude was much different. All I could think was, "Great, that should help. But now the bar has been set and the next thing I write has to be better than the last. How do I make sure I get better? How do I grow as a writer?"

When I see a 4-star review all I see is room for improvement. I live in fear of disappointing readers, so I'm always pushing myself to get better, and hopefully, in doing so, reach a wider audience.

So to answer your question, great reviews are nice, and I'm delighted people enjoy the work. But in my mind all it really means is that the bar has been set higher, and it's my job to clear it.

CP: As with *Fragile Dreams* and *Sacculina*, two of your works we previously reviewed, it is evident that your ability to handle characters and visual imagery is unrivaled. This technique carries on into *Behold the Void*. How do you handle your characters and settings with such depth, and what processes go into bringing them to life?

PF: Thank you for saying that. Yes, I focus a lot on character in my stories. I think it adds empathy and emotion when you feel for a character that's going through something dramatic or terrifying. If you don't care about someone, it makes the story less impactful, so I take my time with development.

One thing I've learned about myself is that I'm pretty good at voices. Personalities. I've got an army in my head ready to go, it's just a matter of picking the right character and seeing what they can do. I'm as surprised as anyone at some of the things my characters think, or how they act in a certain situation. I suppose it's really about visualization. If I can put myself into someone's head, and into a specific situation, from there on out it's just recording what I see, what I hear, what I feel. It's inherent, I think. One of those things you just discover you have. A talent. That said, I can't play instruments or learn foreign languages.

CP: Something that you do as an author that we have rarely seen, is change your writing style drastically to fit into the narrative in which you are telling. Even when your stories are in third person, you still manage to invoke the setting, and often geographical location of the story into your language, like in *Behold the Void's* "The Baby Farmer." Can you tell us a little about the malleability you have in your writing? The decisions you make regarding the language?

PF: I think tone is the most important element of any story. Whether it be a short story, novel or screenplay. It's the first thing I decide before starting a project. And with prose, the style in which you write has a massive impact on tone. "Altar" is very visual, and the tone is nostalgic. "Mother" is a modern gothic, so the dialogue is a bit more formal, the descriptions more dense.

"The Baby Farmer" is essentially a period piece, a story about a woman (serial killer Amelia Dyer) who lived at the turn of the century. I decided the best way to capture her was to let her talk directly to the readers, which is why the framework of the story is built around her journal entries. I also researched actual letters and diary entries from her I was able to find online, and duplicated nuances of both her personality and writing style into the story. Small things, like the fact she tended to ramble and use little punctuation, or never wrote "and," just "a"; to larger things, like the fact that she was protective of her grown daughter, despite having killed hundreds of infants. Again, it allowed some empathy for me, and hopefully for the reader, to present her more fully, and, in this case, as she really was.

CP: Your stories often cross between weird fiction, dark fiction, horror, and stronger themes of a literary nature. *Fragile Dreams* and *Behold the Void's* "Mother" held a more realistic approach, while *Sacculina* and stories from *Behold the Void* such as "Coffin" and "Altar" cross the genres aforementioned. Do you find varying interests in all of these genres? Or do the stories usually evolve on their own?

PF: I don't think about classification at all when telling a story. Other than, "This is a horror story." The stories tell themselves, and the chips fall where they may as to how the story might be described or classified. I just wrote a piece called "Shiloh" that I fully intended to be a more thoughtful, slow-paced, quiet story with a kind of duotone feel, versus Technicolor, if that makes sense. But beta readers keep telling me how relentless and fast-paced it is, which was a huge surprise to me. So it's really out of my hands, I guess.

CP: Writing scripts for films and founding your own bookstore are among the many achievements you've had. One might say you are a jack of all trades. Do you have a singular passion that is stronger than any others? Where do you see yourself in the next twenty years in terms of career path and aspirations?

PF: I've lived a lot of lives. I started in the film industry early on, then I was a music executive for seven years, then started my own business—a bookstore and publishing company—which I ran for seven or eight years, then worked for a marketing agency for a while, and now I'm back full-time in the film industry.

But during all that time, and all those careers, I never stopped writing. It has always been my passion and my dream. I spent decades writing literary short stories, and even wrote three novels. And I've been writing screenplays since 2011, and in that time have had two scripts produced—one for Disney and one, a thriller, for Lifetime.

It wasn't until I started writing genre fiction in 2015 that things have left the station in the prose world. And to answer your question, that's my primary focus now. I'm still writing screenplays, and have a couple very exciting projects in the early stages, but my long-term goal is absolutely to make a career out of writing horror fiction. In the last 2 years I've published two novellas, a collection, and have sold over a dozen stories. I've also found an agent, who is currently shopping a novel and a second collection. So things have gone okay so far.

I look at the careers of guys like Laird Barron, Adam Nevill, Paul Tremblay, Ronald Malfi . . . guys who are making a living from the work, and I see a potential future. That's really my ultimate goal—not to be rich or famous, not to win awards and all that stuff, but to be good enough, and read widely enough, and be prolific enough, to be able to write for a living. But to reach that goal will take a lot of work, a lot of perseverance, and, frankly, a good chunk of luck. So I'll keep my head down, keep doing the work as best I know how, keep pushing myself out there, and keep my fingers crossed. After that, it's out of my hands.

CP: You mentioned earlier that you are often surprised at the evolution of your characters, the old term "a book writes itself" coming to mind. The climactic final novella in *Behold the Void*, *Mandala*, is a jarring, exciting, and emotional journey. Your ability to throw characters into simple situations that become outright terrifying is prevalent throughout the collection, putting ordinary people into extraordinary situations. Could you delve a little into techniques you have when developing tension in a story? Any golden rules of thumb you use when creating these situations?

PF: I think a lot of building tension is *feel.* In other words, having a good feel for how far to go with a scene before cutting away, or changing POV. I like to "cut away" from a scene when it's getting to a burning point of tension. If done correctly, switching POV during a particularly tense sequence can be a lot of fun for the reader. I do this in MANDALA, and also in ALTAR.

It also has a lot to do with pacing. If you're writing to build tension, you might want to speed up the pace by using cleaner, shorter sentences, less description, etc. You don't want to have your hero tied to the conveyor belt while the giant, screaming buzzsaw is getting closer and closer to his heels . . . and then write a couple long, languid sentences about the history of the mill. Or maybe you do. Extending those moments can be delicious, as long as you don't overdo it. Again, terrible answer I know, but it's really a "feel" thing.

So, short answer, mechanically speaking: quicker pacing in the language and strategic cutaways are two of the tricks I employ.

CP: Staying on the topic of character, many believe that the heart of horror or dark fiction lies in character-driven studies. Why do you think this is so much more prevalent—than say, science fiction or fantasy where the worlds are at the epicenter—in the darker realms of literature?

PF: I think horror relies heavily on psychological aspects, much moreso than any other genre. In horror, its vital that you know what a person is thinking and feeling in order to bring the reader into the world you're creating. A big part of writing horror is to make a reader scared, or uncomfortable, or thrilled. And unless the reader can truly identify with the characters in a story, they're not going to feel those things as strongly as you'd like.

A good plot can bring tears, or tension, or joy . . . but you have to go deeper if you want to bring chills, or a sense of danger, or even outright terror. You can't rely on plot alone, you need to make sure the reader feels what the characters are feeling and understand what's going on inside their heads. You need to get a reader involved emotionally. Look, I can write a scene about a hundred spiders eating the flesh off a screaming child, and that's great fun, right? But if the reader just spent some time getting to know that child—learning how he thinks and feels, what he likes or dislikes, his plans for the future—then those spider bites are gonna hurt a little bit more. You'll *feel* it, and hopefully it will haunt you.

CP: You spoke of your experience in the film industry. Can you tell us how, if at all, working with film and penning scripts has helped your writing? If so, do you think it has made the act of writing fiction easier or more difficult?

PF: I think scriptwriting has a lot to offer prose writers. There is a ton of great knowledge about how to construct a 3-Act story, character arcs, building tension and conflict, etc. Also, screenwriting is very visual and dialogue-oriented. A screenplay needs to—very sparsely—give detailed visuals and action, so a director or producer can visualize everything quickly and easily. And the dialogue is a massive element of a script. It needs to convey so much—how a person thinks, what kind of a person they are; it needs to convey emotion, and information. Lastly, dialogue needs to be *unique* to each character. The cowboy at the bar uses different words and has a different speaking style than the big-city lawyer, or the single mom with three kids, or the homeless guy living under the steps, etc.

So yeah, I think scriptwriting taught me a lot about structure, and character, and dialogue for sure, as well as being visceral with descriptions of people and places.

That all said, there are some things you need to *unlearn* when going from script to prose. Especially with novel writing. There are different rules for POV's and scene structure that is way too extensive to get into here, but if there's one thing I've learned it's that knowing all the rules and techniques for short stories, novels and screenplays are great to have in the toolbox, but ultimately they are very much three different art forms, and each has its own methodology you have to adhere to.

CP: We were speaking of your style earlier, and I wanted to focus on the unique aspects of your writing. While reading these three works of yours, we couldn't really compare the style to anything we had read before. The pace is fluid, the imagery vivid and alive, though executed with sharp, concise language that is often poetic, often straightforward. Do you have any major inspirations as an author? Any writers whom you feel factored into your choices of technique and language?

PF: There are a lot of authors I enjoy reading, but there are only a handful of authors who inspire my technique, or language, or style, however you want to coin it. I always mention Laird Barron, who taught me both through his writing and through many conversations about the work. The things he does with language are mind-bending. I also take lessons from Ralph Robert Moore, a favorite of mine. His work taught me about brutality, physicality and sensuality, and how to use it to sweeten a story. Brian Evenson is the master of the unhinged, and no one is better at creating a genuine unease and a disassociated sense of tension. I read poets like Frank Stafford, Charles Simic, Kenneth Patchen, Anne Sexton, and countless others. All of them are great resources for how to use language toward different ends. Lastly, I'd throw Dennis Lehane and Raymond Chandler, Hemingway and Faulkner into the mix, for different reasons but they're all a small part of my prose or the way I choose to structure a story.

CP: You mentioned a novel and a second collection in the works. Can you possibly give us any information on those endeavors to look forward to in the future?

PF: The working title of the novel is A CHILD ALONE WITH STRANGERS, and it's being shopped right now by my agent. It's straight-down-the-middle old-school horror, with some (hopefully) intense emotional elements. It's likely at least a year or two away, seeing as how we haven't sold it yet.

Regarding the collection, it's hard to say. I have a mock ToC of stories that I feel really good about, but it will likely be sold as part of a package with the novel, or put out separately at a date, and with a publisher, to be determined. I'd like to think that I'm sort of in the eye of the storm right now, as I've had a lot of output and now I have to wait and see how things shake out, then hopefully I'll get back to putting stuff out as fast as I can write it. I'm a bit handcuffed at the moment while I try to strategize a bit more of the big career picture. It's frustrating, but exciting as well.

That said, I'll continue putting out stories when able, so hopefully the drought won't be too extensive.

CP: On a final note, many of our readers are writers themselves. We always like to end the interviews with a question for them. Do you have any advice or wisdom you could bestow upon budding writers? Any information you find invaluable in the industry?

PF: I think the biggest piece of advice is to keep a steady ship. Don't get high on the highs or low on the lows. Don't get overly-discouraged by rejections, or if things aren't moving as quickly as you'd like. Perseverance is the name of the game. Slow and steady wins the race. Keep your head down, do the work, and keep grinding.

Also, be professional and courteous. Accept rejections and criticisms graciously, don't push your work on folks too hard, and be kind to others in the field. It's a pretty great community, but like any community, it takes time to fully integrate. I'm still in the early stages myself.

Lastly, be yourself. Be true to your voice. Not everyone is gonna like what you do (some are gonna hate it), but that's part of the business of any artist. It's all subjective, and people will have their opinions. That's why they call it Art. But if you work hard, and keep at it, you'll find your audience, and then the real fun begins.

INSIDE THE SHADOW BOOTH with Dan Coxon

(Originally published in the Gehenna Post)

Greetings from the Nether Realm,

We are delighted to present our interview with award-winning editor Dan Coxon, discussing his new project *The Shadow Booth*, which is currently active as a Kickstarter. We encourage each and everyone one of you to support this venture, as Dan is a close friend to G&H and he also will soon be offering a few of our publications as tiers in the crowdfunding project.

Alas, let's begin!

CP: *The Shadow Booth* is an exciting venture, and also something to look forward to for all readers of Dark Fiction and Weird Fiction. What were some of the key inspirations behind developing this project?

DC: In all honesty, it's not something I was planning to do. But I was going out to a lot of live reading events, and talking to a lot of writers, and it became clear to me that there's an abundance of wonderful weird and eerie fiction out there that's struggling to find a home. I run my own proofreading and editorial services company (*Momus Editorial*) so I'm used to putting books together for other people, and getting them to a professional standard, ready for print. It seemed a small step to start doing that for myself rather than for someone else—and to give these great stories a home. At the same time, I didn't want it to be just another horror magazine. The stories I love are generally strange and unsettling rather than outright horror. Sometimes this means they fall within the horror genre, but at other times they don't. If a story leaves the reader unsettled and uneasy, then it's right for *The Shadow Booth*.

CP: In the Kickstarter, you mention that you are trying to end the trend of non-paying markets. Can you go a little into the background of this trend for our readers, and how it is affecting authors?

DC: Calling it a trend probably makes it sound more ominous than it actually is, but I certainly think there's a worrying tendency to see writing as 'content' rather than creative work, and to assume that writers don't need paying. Most authors spend a huge amount of time writing and crafting their stories, so to have an editor or publisher assume that they should be able to publish it for free strikes me as dismissive and slightly insulting. I used to work as a freelance journalist, and I saw the same thing happening there. There's sometimes this deluded attitude that they're somehow doing the writer a favor by giving their work exposure. They're not. If someone truly values your work, they will pay for it.

CP: If everything goes according to plan, what do you see in the future of *Shadow Booth*? Do you plan more volumes?

DC: The initial idea was for it to be a bi-annual journal. I'm going to stick with that for now, and see how it works out. Volume 2 will hopefully be out next summer, and Volume 3 again next winter. One of the inspirations for the look and feel of it was the *Pan Books of Horror*, and I liked the way they kept coming, to produce a series. We'll see.

CP: Literary Journals are far and in-between these days. Why did you decide on a journal instead of a magazine?

DC: I'll confess that I'm not always clear on the distinction! Some publications that I consider to be journals advertise themselves as magazines, while some magazines claim to be journals. I definitely wanted to produce something in book format though, rather than a magazine. I think it encourages people to take the writing more seriously, and it's a format that's nicer to read. Plus, it looks good on your shelves, and hopefully has a longer shelf life. In fact, I considered calling it an anthology, but that didn't seem to convey the sense that it would be coming out twice a year. So, basically, it was a decision based on snobbery.

CP: There are a lot of heavyweight authors involved in this project. Did you and the writers find common grounds in the aspirations for *Shadow Booth*?

DC: Filling the first volume proved to be ridiculously easy. What was more difficult was saying no to a couple of excellent authors, whose stories weren't quite right for the tone I'm trying to achieve. I was amazed at how positive the reaction was, and how quickly most of the writers 'got' the concept. In fact, most of them already had something suitable written, just waiting to find a home.

CP: What inspired the title "Shadow Booth?" How does it factor in to the themes and purpose of the literary journal?

DC: That's a tough one. I was just playing around with images and words in my head, very early on in the process. I wanted to reflect the dark, unsettling subject matter, which was where the 'Shadow' came from. But then I had an image in my head of something like an old fairground puppet booth, like the Punch & Judy booths you get here in England. There's something quite creepy about them, quite playful but also edgy, as if anything might happen. I liked that. Interestingly, since settling on the title I've read two stories by Thomas Ligotti that feature puppet booths—so clearly I'm not the first to find them a little weird!

CP: Undertaking the editing and marketing for a project like this can be very time consuming. If everything pans out, will you continue other ventures as you have done in the past? If so, do you have any other projects in the works that our readers can look forward to?

DC: I'll still be running my editorial services company, which is what pays the bills. I'll also be writing stories all the time—I've been doing that too long to be able to stop now. I write mainstream literary fiction under my own name, and darker fictions under the name Ian Steadman. I'm also a Contributing Editor at *The Lonely Crowd*, an excellent literary journal here in the UK, which I'll continue to work on. I'll find the time somehow!

CP: With the recent advent of a surge in popularity of Weird Fiction and Dark Fiction, could you maybe delve a little bit into why you believe these genres are coming back to the forefront in recent years?

DC: It's interesting, isn't it. It's something that seems to be happening across the board, from books to films to TV.

If I wanted to analyze it in depth, I think there's a case to be made for it being a product of the current political climate, and our fears for what the future holds. The news seems to be getting darker and weirder every day, and there's a growing sense of terrible things brewing that are beyond our control. That plays straight into the arms of the weird and the eerie. But at the same time, I genuinely believe these things come in cycles, as most things do. Maybe its time had simply come.

CP: Finally, I wanted to ask what ways our readers can help with this project. What links can they share, how can they get the word out, etc. At G&H, we celebrate Dark/Weird Fiction and more importantly, the authors behind the works. So let us know how we can do our part!

DC: First and foremost, please order a copy of Volume 1! We're still crowdfunding until October 25th, and this only works if we meet our target. In fact, I'm hoping to go a little over target, to make Volume 2 a little easier. Many people are opposed to supporting crowdfunded projects on the basis that they're asking for handouts, but we're not—we really just want people to order a copy of the journal. If you decide to go a bit further a grab a T-shirt, or a story critique, or a parcel of signed books, then that's great. But even then, I hope you'll be getting value for your money. We don't want charity. Beyond that (and once you've backed us!) please tell people about it, follow us on Twitter and Facebook, share the links. Getting the word out is half the struggle.

The crowdfunding page is here:
https://www.kickstarter.com/projects/dan-coxon/the-shadow-booth-a-new-journal-of-weird-and-eerie

And these are our social media pages:
https://twitter.com/TheShadowBooth
https://www.facebook.com/TheShadowBooth

You can also find us at:
http://www.theshadowbooth.com

LIMBS

By Jim Horlock

I hear Them all the time.

All day the sound of Them fills the city. Howling, gibbering calls that echo around inside my skull. There's no traffic anymore. No noisy engines. Most generators are dead so there's no constant background hum of electrics. No bustling human crowd either. The sounds of Them travel a long way in the quiet. I can't escape them, no matter where I go, no matter what I stuff my ears with. High-pitched wails and grotesque cat-calls made by vocal chords stretched to the maximum and beyond. Or worse—if there's one thing I've learned since all this started it's that there's always worse.

The worst are the ones that still sound human. A little girl lost, screaming for her parents. A mother weeping with broken-hearted sobs. Cries of anger so close to normal that you could almost believe them. Until you realise that sound is coming from a mouth with too many teeth or a throat longer than your arm. These sounds are a mirage of an oasis to a man dying of thirst—the promise of hope. The truth is hard and sharp as a knife between the ribs: there aren't any people left here. Every day I'm getting closer to certain that I'm the last one. There is no hope.

I sight one of Them through the scope of my rifle. It can't see me; I've picked out my position on the roof for that exact reason. It looks damaged, like it might have been in a fight, but it's hard to know for sure. I've seen Them fight each other before but not often. It's dragging two of its legs behind it and it's unsteady on the others, resulting in a strange, shambling gait. It's leaving a trail of some dark fluid, smears and spatters on the abandoned pavement. Could be blood. Could be some kind of mucus. You can't ever be sure with Them. I saw one once that spun webs like a spider. The strands had little bits of bone, chips of teeth and fingernails stuck in them. Webs made from people it had eaten.

The thing clicks its teeth together mindlessly as it stumbles onwards and I feel my anger building—a bottled thunderstorm in my core. Sometimes it's stronger than others, pressed right against the glass. Sometimes I barely notice it. But it's always there.

They've taken everything from me. *Everything.* I can taste the hate at the back of my throat like acid. It crawls up to the bridge of my nose and makes my eyes water. There's no words for the intensity of the loathing I feel. I wonder: how many people has this one killed?

My finger tightens on the trigger and my breath hisses through the bars of my teeth. My bullet would splatter its head before it had any clue what was happening. I could kill it with a simple squeeze. Bam. One less of Them in the world.

It takes a lot of effort to ease my finger back off the trigger. Killing it won't make me less angry and the sound of the shot will almost certainly alert others to my presence. There might be hundreds of them, thousands, lurking in the nearby buildings, wandering mindlessly around until they catch any sign of prey. They find us by sound, by sight or by scent. It's too much of a risk to kill this one and it will gain me nothing.

Keep calm, think logical. Anger only gets you killed.

I watch the thing down my scope as it passes over the empty street, between twin rows of dust-coated cars long out of use. It meanders through the trash, the upturned bins and dented shopping trolleys. I watch it until it's out of sight.

Never take your eyes off them.

"Just animals," I mutter to myself. "They're just animals."

It's not really a comfort. They're not 'just' anything. They're the catastrophe that destroyed the world. They're the deaths of millions.

The sun is well on its way to meet the horizon and I can't afford to be out at night. During the day it's a risk, albeit a calculated one. At night it would be suicide.

At night the gas will roll back in.

Jack always said it comes in at night due to the drop in temperature but he knew more about gas and its behaviour than I do. I just took his word for it and make sure I'm always in before dark.

A part of me wants to go out all day and kill as many as I can, like the guy from *I Am Legend* but I know if I do that I'll go mad. This isn't about revenge, it can't be. It's about survival. That's why I have to tell myself they're 'just animals' when I know really they're much more. Life is hard and it doesn't care about revenge. There are no natural laws of justice. There is only survival of the fittest, and if I want to survive I have to be as hard and cold as life is.

My current base is in a storage centre, like one of those ones from the auction shows on TV. It was Jack's idea and it had proved to be a good one. The security on the building was good and there were hundreds of units full of supplies. People had stored clothes, blankets, camping equipment. One guy had even stored a bunch of tin food. He was probably one of those survivalist nuts planning for the apocalypse. The irony wasn't lost on me as I helped myself.

Best of all is the security office. It has a heavy door, a comfy chair and dozens of CCTV screens showing almost every inch of the building and the perimeter. I don't sleep much but what little rest I do get, I get in that chair, secure in the knowledge that I'll be able to see something coming as soon as I wake.

I bolt the door behind me and sit down, laying my rifle across my lap. A quick glance at my emergency go-bag confirms that it's still in place and untouched, ready for me to grab if I need to make a quick exit. The glances at the bag started as a paranoid twitch but have become a relied-on trait. Too many times I've been forced to make a panicked escape from a hideout and been left with no supplies, forced to start over again.

The bag contains some tinned food, a good knife, a handgun and some ammo, blankets, a compass, a city map, a first aid kit and a few other odds and ends. It also contains my only photo of Julia, taken from a frame, lined with creases and folds and jammed into the box of the first aid kit. Not exactly a great way to honour her memory. It's too painful to look at but I can't throw it away either. That would be like she never existed. I threw away the ultrasound and regretted it every day since.

The rain comes in hard and there's a rumble of thunder. The storm clouds bring the night in quicker and the sound of rain hammering the metal roof makes me edgy. It's too much like the sound of hundreds of running footsteps. I press the flaps of my hat against my ears (I'm not going to be able to hear danger coming over the rain anyway) and blink the tiredness out of my eyes. I don't want to sleep. Sleep is where memories catch up with you and hold you prisoner.

The rain does a good job of blocking the external cameras as well as deafening me but I keep a fevered eye on them regardless, gaze flicking from one to the next in a now all-too-familiar pattern. For a moment, I think I see something in the corner of the car park near the fence but there's too many droplets on the lens to tell. It could just be a distortion.

I used to keep an eye out for Jack. He knew the city well. He'd almost certainly return here. I'd seen so many others come and go but Jack had always been so calm and certain. He was a hunter and grew up around guns, tracking wild animals with his dad out in Canada. He knew how to survive.

"They're just animals," he'd say. "You've got to treat them that way. Dangerous, sure. But just animals. Animals can be avoided. Animals can be killed. They don't strategise. You've just gotta stay smart about it."

It's hard to believe he could be gone too.

I feel myself starting to drift, so I shift in the chair, shaking my head abruptly to try and throw off the heavy drowsiness. I know I can't fight it forever but I also know that every moment I'm asleep is a moment that I'm vulnerable. It was so much easier when there were two of us. Always one to keep watch.

I loved to watch her sleep.

It started out as an over-protective thing. As soon as she fell pregnant I became one of those expectant fathers that freaks whenever his partner stubs their toe or tries to lift so much as a shoebox. It irritated her at first but she soon fell into teasing me about it. Julia was like that. So easy-going. Always poking fun at me but never hurting my feelings.

I'd had these nightmares that she'd stop breathing in her sleep, so I started waking up all the time to check on her. My eyes would snap open every half hour or so like clockwork and I'd listen for her breathing. Then I'd check on her anyway to make sure it wasn't my own breath I could hear. Not that there was much doubt. Since she hit her second trimester she started snoring like a trooper.

After a while the paranoia about her dying in her sleep faded. I kept checking her because it'd become a habit but also just because I liked to see her looking so peaceful. Even with her mouth wide open and a sound like an angry engine coming out of her nose, she still looked beautiful.

That night though, she was restless. Her face creased with worry in her sleep. Or was it pain? She moaned and grunted and suddenly sat bolt-upright, clutching her swollen belly.

"What's wrong?" I asked immediately. Since we started coming closer to the due date, I was constantly on alert for the start of her contractions. I had an emergency bag stowed in the car, ready to go. She thought it was ridiculous; she was still weeks away yet.

"It hurts," she said, her teeth gritting, her back bowing forward over her stomach, both arms wrapped around herself. "It hurts a lot."

"Is it contractions?" I asked. "Do we need to go to the hospital?"

"No, I don't think so—"

The words were barely out of her mouth when she let out a sharp cry and her legs kicked under the blanket.

"Okay, we're going," I said, leaping from the bed.

"It's not contractions," she said, rolling her eyes.

"I don't care. If it hurts this much, I'm taking you to the hospital."

I snap awake with a snort, suddenly aware that I'd been unconscious. In a panic, my senses bombard me with information that might pertain to any immediate danger. My eyes check the corners of the room (clear), the ceiling (clear), the door (still bolted). My ears pick up the dull drumming (just the rain on the roof). My nose picks up a musty smell (just my own unwashed clothes).

As my breathing slows again I lower the rifle gently. With the momentary panic over, my thoughts return to the dream. We'd heard about the gas, of course. They were just vague reports then, on the nightly news. No-one was really sure what it was, save for that the orange-coloured fog only appeared at night, in random areas around the country, and that it caused massive communication problems with every area it hit. We didn't know back then that the communication problems were caused by there being no-one left to communicate with.

Some thought it was a natural phenomenon, some kind of new pollen or even swarms of insects. Others thought it was the result of man-made chemicals interacting with the atmosphere. Of course, the chemtrail crazies thought it was a government conspiracy of one kind or another. Either way, it wasn't a major worry for us. We lived in a nice suburban neighbourhood. We didn't think anything could really harm us. It was the same lie everyone tells themselves in that situation. We're safe. It'll never happen to us.

Nobody's safe. That's the real lesson I've learnt from all this. Life is cruel and nobody's safe. Not even people as mentally strong and well-prepared as Jack.

I shoot a look at the external cameras again. The distortion from earlier is gone and I think it was a raindrop smearing the lens but it still makes me uneasy. I can't see any of Them and I don't see Jack either. Even now there's a part of me that clings to the desperate wish to see his hybrid pulling quietly into the car park. He'd painted it matte black and coated the windows in something to take the shine out of the glass. So long as he kept under a certain speed, the petrol engine didn't kick in and the car was almost silent.

We'd used it for night runs a bunch of times. They were less active at night and the gas masks he'd taken from wherever-the-hell people got gas masks from protected us from the sinister orange cloud. We still tried to avoid it wherever we could, though. There was no sense chancing fate.

Sometimes we saw it rolling over a part of the city like a wave of sunset mist. Except that sounds beautiful and this thing was nothing but a mass of ugliness, a foulness, a thick, choking fog that oozed its way over buildings and down streets with an almost palpable malevolence. I couldn't help but personify it, assigning it traits and calling it names. Evil, I'd designate it. Alien. Malicious. I'd catch myself swearing under my breath when I saw it, not out of fear or awe but out of sheer undiluted hatred.

Jack would caution me when I spoke that way, interrupting my string of curses with a long stare.

"All that emotion ain't gonna get you anywhere but dead," he'd say. "And I won't be taken with you. Life's easier with a partner but don't think I won't cut you loose if you can't keep it together. Keep calm, think logical. The fog ain't nothing but fog."

I'd calm myself down grudgingly and settle back into keeping an eye on the distant cloud.

Once parts of the electric grid went down and the city was plunged into darkness, Jack became more eager to do our supply runs at night. He was certain the things had no real night-vision.

"It's in their behaviour," he'd say. "They don't hunt at night because they're no good at it."

I didn't take much reassurance from that but I'd learned that doing what Jack said kept me alive.

Funny thing about the colour orange; if there's no light to shine on it, it just looks black, same as any other colour. So when we were raiding a local food store in the dark, we didn't see the cloud until it was almost on us.

I freaked when I saw the darkness seep through the door, a patch of pure night.

"Masks!" Jack barked, his orders overriding my panic and talking directly to my muscles, which propelled me to grab my mask and slip it on. I also grabbed my gun, as though shooting the gas would do any good. Just holding it made me feel calmer, though. You know things have gone to hell when a thing designed exclusively to kill makes for a good security blanket.

"Steady," Jack warned me as the gas rolled closer.

I could hear my own breathing, amplified and weirdly altered by the filter on the mask. I tried to get it under control but it got faster and faster as the gas rolled right up to us. It was too late to run now. The logical part of my mind told me that the mask would save me, but I'd seen what the gas could do and I was terrified.

Then it engulfed us and I lost sight of everything else. I closed my eyes tight but it made no difference whether they were open or closed; inside the gas cloud, the darkness was total.

"Jack?" I called out. I kept my voice low, despite my fear. I didn't want to attract anything that might be listening.

No response.

"Jack?" I called a little louder, straining my ears to hear any sign of him, trying to force my hearing to increase.

Still nothing.

He had been standing pretty close when the gas hit but maybe the thickness of the cloud was insulating the sound somehow?

Carefully I moved, trying to picture the room as it was before it became a pitch black nightmare. Jack had been standing by the shelves, only about ten feet away.

I reached out one hand and found the shelf. My arm was shaking. I couldn't help but think about what would happen if I reached out and touched one of Them, something awful and twisted standing so close to me but hidden by the gas.

I had to force myself to take every single step as I moved along the shelves, sliding my hand over the wood. Even the noise of my glove on the shelf and the sound of my boots creaking sounded incredibly loud. My feet didn't want to move but I made them.

There was no sign of Jack.

I don't know how long I stood there for. Eventually the gas rolled on, like it always does, and the clear air it left behind confirmed that I was alone. I was never sure what happened to Jack. Had he finally cut me loose after realising I was no real use to him? Had he simply up and left me in the orange mist? Or had something taken him? Had one of Them snatched him without a sound, missing me by pure chance?

I don't think I'll ever know.

The hybrid was still parked outside but Jack had the keys so I had to walk back to the storage centre. It took hours of careful, tense movements to cross a distance of only a few blocks. I hadn't been so afraid since that museum . . .

I wake with a start, gunfire from that terrible night ringing in my ears.

For a moment, I see the dark horror-filled corridors of the museum in front of me as though I'm there before the dream fades and reality takes hold.

It takes me a heartbeat to realise that the banging hasn't stopped and another to recognise that it isn't gunfire at all but something banging hard at the metal roof.

Frantic, I check the CCTV screens just in time to see one of them lose signal as the ceiling it was attached to caves in under the assault from the outside.

I grab my go-bag and my gun but don't head for the exit just yet. I could be running straight into Them if I don't plan this. Instead I hover in front of the CCTV screens, like an agitated fly eager to escape a glass bottle.

I need to know where they are and how many. If it's just one I might be able to take it down and continue using this place as my base.

Whatever it is, it's fast. I can't catch anything on the cameras but a pale blur, thundering its way along the corridors. It seems to be running blind though, which means it doesn't necessarily know I'm in here.

A strange creaking sound makes me turn and what I see makes me raise my gun in panic.

There are fingers slipping beneath the bottom of the security door, curling up to take hold of the wood. Dozens of them, all along the gap between door and floor, as though a whole group of people are impossibly lying on top of one another in the small corridor beyond. The fingers take firm grip and begin to pull at the wood.

I'm out of there before it gets through the door but only just. I can hear the wood splintering and a horrible hungry gargling noise behind me as I slam the roof hatch shut. Jack put this escape route into place not long after we moved in. He never bedded down in a place unless he knew he could get out again in a hurry. I'd never had to use it before though.

Keep calm, keep calm, I have to remind myself. It's not easy when you know these things are after you. *Don't run blind. Don't make mistakes.*

I move as quickly as I can across the rain-slick rooftop, glancing over my shoulder constantly for any sign of it. How did it know I was in there? It came straight to the security office once it was inside. *No time to think about that now. Get to the ladder, get to the street.*

The rain is still hammering and it drives into my eyes, making it hard to see. Twice my feet almost slip out from under me as I try to strike a balanced pace between quick and quiet but I make it to the ladder that runs down the back wall of the building to the floor.

For a moment, I think there might be more of Them waiting for me in the dark below. There are no street lights covering the area and I dare not use my torch in case it gives away my position to any others that might be nearby. I don't have a choice now. There's no other way off the roof except back the way I came and the thing that broke through my door is bound to follow me up here at any minute.

I steel myself and start to climb down the ladder.

I'm not even halfway down when the metal groans. I freeze up, gripping the cold wet rungs for dear life, but it's too late. There's nothing I can do as the ladder peels away from the wall except cry out in fear.

They saw Julia pretty quickly when we got to the hospital.

One nurse fussed around her in the room while the other asked me questions outside the door. Now we were surrounded by medical staff and high-tech equipment; I was starting to relax. Everything would be okay.

An emergency announcement over the Tannoy system warned us that the gas was coming but we thought we'd got the window closed in time. I'm still not sure why whatever wisp of the stuff that got into the room affected only her. Maybe she was in a weakened state, what with the pregnancy. Maybe the air currents just took it that way. I didn't even realise it was the gas at first; I thought it was something wrong with the baby.

It started with convulsions. Her back arched, her legs kicked out and her arms flailed at her sides. Her eyes rolled back in her head. I was screaming for help even though the nurses were already in the room. They shouted medical jargon back and forth and attended to Julia as I stood there helpless.

Two doctors rushed in as her throat started to swell up. Within seconds it was like she'd swallowed a tennis ball whole.

"We're going to need to intubate!" shouted one of the doctors. "Airway's obstructed!"

The nurses were holding her down now, her convulsions were so violent.

Outside the window, the orange fog looked on.

Even through her swollen throat, her scream was terrible. There was an awful crunch, like a fistful of walnuts snapping, and blood sprayed across the ceiling.

A hand reached out from inside her.

At first, I thought it was the baby. I watched it grow, the arm rising like a tree in one of those sped-up footage pieces from a nature documentary, a long pale limb, adult and fully formed, with a handful of writhing fingers at the end, rising straight from the hole in her chest.

The doctors and nurses had stopped working on her. We were all frozen in place as more of these limbs tore their way through her torso, reaching up towards the ceiling. Her body rose from the bed almost gracefully, her natural arms and legs hanging limp as more of these aberrant limbs burst from her back, lifting her from the blood-soaked mattress.

The many hands manoeuvred themselves, passing her weight between them until they'd twisted her around in the air face down. Suddenly her head snapped up to look at one of the doctors. Her expression was twisted into something savage, something hateful. I'd never seen her look like that.

She gave an inhuman snarl as the limbs propelled her from the bed in a feral pounce and she bore one of the women to the floor, dozens of hands tearing at her, beating her and all the while the thing that had been Julia yelped and howled.

I was terrified.

The doctor was dead in seconds, beaten to a bloody pulp. Julia leaped at one of the stunned nurses next. I remember noting numbly that some of the doctor's hair was still clumped in several of her new hands.

The nurses scream woke my body into action. I made no conscious decisions but my legs propelled me from the room. I slammed the door behind me and pressed my back hard against it to keep it closed. There were shrieks and cries coming from elsewhere in the building but I didn't really register them. I became aware of blood on my face and wiped it away, looking down at red fingertips. I wasn't sure whose it was.

The door thudded at my back and I let out an unconscious whimper, pressing my weight against it. It banged again, the sound accompanied by a strange gargling whine. She was trying to get out. My wife was a monster, she'd killed everyone in the room and now she was trying to get out. Trying to get me.

I break the surface of the nightmare-memory with a gasp, lashing out at the past before realising I'd been dreaming. My senses filter in almost one at a time as my breathing gradually slows. I hurt all over. I'm lying on something hard and wet. There is rain in my face and blood in my mouth. My brain is pounding and my hand comes away bloody when I touch the back of my head. The paltry sunlight, strained through layers of grey cloud, is still enough to hurt my eyes.

For a moment, I'm not sure what had happened but then I remember my attempted escape from the storage centre and the betrayal of the ladder.

I look up, squinting through the pain, at where the metal had pulled away from the wall. I must have fallen at least twenty feet. How long had I been out for?

In a panic I check my surroundings, each twist of my neck ringing bells of pain up and down my spine. I had landed in the alleyway behind the storage centre, a thin strip of concrete between the building and the fence, the other side of which was a train yard. Had I really been so lucky as to lie here all night and be overlooked? My watch was broken in the fall so I have no idea of the time but it looks to be at least mid-morning.

I can't count on my luck to hold out any longer, though. I need to get out of here as soon as possible and get to new shelter.

As I try to stand, molten agony pours through my left leg and I collapse, hissing, to the ground. It takes several minutes for the pain to fade again, leaving behind a feeling of deep cavernous hopelessness. A busted leg could mean the end of me. I try to stand again and find that I can put only the slightest amount of weight it—anything more is torture. I can't outrun Them like this. My only hope is to find shelter and stay put until I'm healed but I don't even know bad the injury is. Is it just sprained or is this some kind of fracture? Jack would know. I hate him for not being here.

Worse still, my rifle was damaged in the fall, its barrel severely bent. That just leaves me with the handgun in the shoulder holster under my jacket.

Stay calm. Think. Plan. They're just animals and the fog is just fog. They can't strategise—you can. That's how you survive.

I squint up at the clouds, trying to gauge the time of day. My first step to survival is getting somewhere secure as soon as possible.

I use the bent rifle as a kind of walking stick.

With my go-bag slung over my shoulder and my pistol drawn and ready in one hand. A part of me just wants to climb inside one of the cargo carriages and pull the doors shut, wait until night when they're less active. But at night I won't be able to see as well and finding new shelter will be even harder.

The going is painfully slow, literally and figuratively, as I make my way across the train yard. I'm panting hard, which makes it difficult to hear if any of Them are nearby and I'm very aware of how much noise my stumbling footsteps make on the gravel.

I haven't been wounded like this since I escaped the hospital, since I found my way by sheer dumb luck to the museum.

As a stronghold, it had seemed like a good idea.

It was, by nature, a solid structure equipped with great security. It was spacious, heated and, at least in the wing where we made our home, climate controlled, which meant the gas couldn't get in.

I wasn't sure how I'd ended up there. After Julia . . . after she died I'd been a broken man. The people at the museum made me feel welcome. They were a collection of tattered half-families, grizzled loners, and terrified children. But they had ample supplies and they relied on each other. They gave me an area to sleep in and food. They treated my wounds and gave me company. They also gave me a sense a security, which I never thought I'd feel again at that point. I still woke up crying out in fear each night but at least once I was awake, I knew I was safe.

It was at the museum that I heard the most varied theories about the gas. One woman, Caroline, had been a lab-tech at a water treatment plant and was a keen scientist. She had read an article about a radical new treatment in development for amputees that proposed to use stem cells to regrow entire limbs. Caroline was convinced that gas was something to do with that.

Another of the survivors there, Paul, was determined that the gas somehow reactivated what he called 'recombinant DNA,' which he explained as being all the junk in our genes from the various stages of our evolution that just isn't active anymore.

Of course some people thought aliens were to blame, or that it was some kind of terrorist attack, but none of them were as impassioned as Caroline. She was almost manic about it. One of the other women, Janine, told me that Caroline had lost two kids to the gas and they'd killed her husband once it turned them and that it had made her kind of obsessed.

Perhaps that's why we found her one night, smothering the children in their sleep.

The resultant gunfire had broken one of the sturdy windows and the gas, pressed against the glass like some perverted watcher, was free to come rolling in.

The rest of that night had been a nightmare of chaos and panic as we fled from the orange fog. I remember catching a glimpse of Paul, screaming as the gas overwhelmed him. He staggered forward, trying to reach for help as a series of sickening crunches sounded from inside him, each one signalling the change of his joints to a new, inhuman position. A violent convulsion threw him to the ground as his legs bent to new shapes. His face turned to me, the skin writhing like a stormy ocean and blood pooled from his mouth as his teeth fell out.

I shake myself out of the memory. I'm not sure if it's the tiredness, the events of last night or the blood loss that's making it hard to focus on the present, but if I don't stay sharp I'll end up dead.

I come back to reality just in time as I hear one of Them close by, crunching across the gravel. As I freeze in place, crouched against one of the dormant rusting carriages, it stalks into view.

It walks on four legs, the knees of the rear two inverted to make balance easier. Its fore-limbs are more like arms and it carries its weight on worn, flat knuckles in a gorilla-like gait. Where the head would be on any normal quadruped, there is instead another spinal column, curving upwards from the shoulders like a grotesque centaur. This second torso is all but a skeleton, thinly held together by bright red ropes of tendon and muscle. The grisly skull at the summit of the monster is only partially formed and, through the gaps in its cranium, I can see something fleshy beating like a heart.

It turns towards me before I can make a move to hide and I thank god that it has no eyes. Instead it seems to be seeking me out by hearing, tilting its gruesome head to one side. I try not to breathe but it seems to hear me anyway, shuffling slowly closer on two feet and a hand while the other hand crawls its way across the metal wall of the train car.

If I stay here it will find me. If I move it might hear me. No choice.

Moving as slowly and carefully as I can, my heart hammering so loud I'm sure the creature will hear it, I lower myself to the ground. I don't want to take my eyes off it but I have no choice as I'm forced to turn my head to fit under the carriage. I can smell the stink of the creature, old blood and stale piss, looming over me as I painstakingly slide under the metal frame, desperate not to make a noise on the gravel . . .

The sky is much darker by the time I painfully crawl from my hiding place. I'm not sure if it's later than I thought or if the clouds are gathering. Either way, it's not a good sign. I have to make it out of the trainyard and across the highway before I reach even the closest buildings and there's no guarantee any of them will be suitable. Or empty.

By the time I leave the trainyard it's becoming clear I'm not going to make it inside before dark.

The streetlights over the highway have come on (this part of the city evidently still has power) which means dusk can't be far away. I'm exhausted. I need to get somewhere, anywhere, I can rest. I don't know when I last ate, I don't know how much blood I've lost but I know for sure that limping along like this as quietly as I can is sapping what little energy I have.

Even if I could make it to the buildings, it's a painstaking process making sure they're clear and finding a defensible room. I start to get angry. If it hadn't been for that stupid ladder, if I had prepared the escape route better, if I hadn't fallen. I grit my teeth against the parade of torturous ifs circling in my mind. They won't help me now. I need to get out of the open, by any means necessary.

That's when I hear something that makes my blood freeze.

A horrible pattering. Hundreds of hands smacking against the floor. In an instant I'm taken back to the dark corridors of the hospital, the night Julia died.

The power had gone out only a few minutes after the gas rolled in. I'm sure hospitals are supposed to have back-up generators and things like that but they didn't kick in and I was left in the darkness with the screaming.

I'd managed to get away from Julia by shoving a stretcher in front of the door to her room and running as fast as I could. I'd fled blind through the corridors, trying to find my way out but the place was a maze and it was even worse in the dark.

Julia wasn't the only one who'd been changed by the fog. The hospital was a nightmare of frenzied monstrosities. There was blood on the walls. Bodies, beaten and mutilated, were scattered around. I tried not to look at them. Some had tooth marks in their skin. Others were in pieces.

Something awful was happening in paediatrics. I made the mistake of glimpsing in through the glass panel in the door. Most of the corridor was taken up by a large mass, a dark slope with a human torso at its peak, its bald head just a few inches below the tiles of the ceiling.

A flash of light from outside, maybe from a passing car, gave me a glimpse of the abomination.

The lower slopes of the thing writhed, glistening. Hundreds of worms coiled and tangled, slowly slithering over and around each other. Not worms, I realised in a moment of appalling understanding, but guts. The intestines of the thing had spilled and multiplied and now they spread out like questing roots from a macabre tree, slick with blood and mucous.

I watched, cemented in place by horror, as the thing dragged the unconscious body of an orderly, loops of serpentine digestive tract wrapped around his legs. As he disappeared into the mass, the thing let out a long, low, damp moan and a shudder of pleasure.

When I heard the pitter-pattering of dozens of agile hands, I knew she'd come for me. There must have been hundreds of people in the hospital when the gas rolled over it and dozens of those must have been changed by it. The chances of her tracking me down, singling me out of a crowd that size, should have been tiny. I knew she'd find me anyway. I knew it was me she wanted.

I turned from the glass and saw her charging, spider-like down the corridor towards me.

I hobble as fast as I can onto the bus and fold the doors shut behind me.

Dragging myself into the aisle, I duck below the seats and hold my breath, praying that whatever it is, the thing didn't see me. I know it's close; the rapid pat-pat-pat of its feet had been loud before I'd slid behind the bus—hopefully out of sight.

I hold my pistol close, cradling it against my chest. For a moment, I feel like breaking down in tears. The running, the hiding, the constant fear and tension, I just can't take it anymore. This isn't how it was supposed to be. I'm supposed to be with Julia, painting a bedroom blue or pink and getting into arguments at 3AM about whose turn it is to comfort the crying baby. Instead I'm in a constant nightmare where every single thing is twisted and cruel. There's no comfort. There's no hope.

The thing slams itself against the window of the bus and makes me jump.

Four hands with long fingers press against the glass, a pair either side of an emaciated face. I can't tell if it was a man or a woman before it changed. Its eyes have melted away, their jelly staining the withered, hollow cheeks below. It opens its mouth slowly and impossibly wide, its jaw unhinging to dangle in front of its throat. From between two rows of healthy looking human teeth, a tongue the size of my hand emerges. It hits the glass with a muffled wet thud. At the centre of this pock-marked muscle, a single eye flicks open. The tiny pupil fixes on me, practically vibrating with hatred.

The tongue retracts, the jaw crunches back into place and the creature begins beating its fists against the windows and screaming bloody murder.

Suddenly, impossibly, I'm filled with the will to live. It's probably a purely biological reaction to danger. Fight or flight or whatever. Adrenaline pumping into my body. Raw chemistry demanding that I survive this. But it works.

I raise my gun to the monster. As soon as it breaks through, I'll shoot it in the head and get the hell away from here. There's no guarantee that will work on this thing; there may not even be a brain inside that skull but I'll cross that bridge when I come to it.

It's then that I realise the thing outside the window isn't my biggest problem.

It's the gas.

The gas is pouring between the buildings like a tidal wave and it's finally got me trapped.

Panicking, I forget my gun and fumble in my go-bag for the mask. My frantic heartbeat drowns out the pounding on the windows. I pull the gasmask free from the go-bag's other contents and the bottom drops out of my stomach.

The filter is broken. Part of it falls away as I lift the mask up. I must have broken it when I fell from the rooftop.

I look back to the windows, now webbed with cracks from the beating they've taken. Any second now the creature will smash them and the gas will pour in. There's nothing I can do.

The gas knows it too. It spreads around the bus slowly, like an octopus around a bottle with a fish trapped inside. I can sense its smug satisfaction. It's waited all this time for me. It knew I'd never escape.

The glass shatters and the gas oozes its way in, crawling over the seats towards me. I shuffle backwards as far as I can, frantic to keep out of its reach but I know it's no good. All I can do is take one last breath of non-lethal air and hold it as long as possible.

I can't see or hear the creature anymore. The unwelcome embrace of the orange fog has become my whole world. My lungs burn as I try to keep it from entering me—another hopeless act of defiance—but I can't hold my breath forever.

The first deep gasp brings searing pain almost instantly.

My throat slams shut like a trap, preventing me from screaming but the gas is already inside. My bones feel like they're melting. My skin bubbles as I start to fit, limbs in spasm.

In my last moments, I think of Julia.

I think of the smell of her hair and how it came out in bloody clumps.

I think of the feel of her skin, her fingers around my throat, choking the life out of me.

I think of her big brown eyes. I remember how one of them was knocked from its socket as I caved in her skull with a fire extinguisher.

I have nothing left. Not my memories. Not my own body.

As the pain reaches a point beyond anything I've ever known, I feel a hand pushing at my chest.

Pushing from the inside.

Some say **Jim Horlock** was forged from mankind's fascination with darkness and that his sole purpose is to terrify and tantalise. They postulate that he is an anthropomorphized entity, bound in human flesh and driven only to spread fear. Others say that is ridiculous and that he's a 29-year-old writer from Wales, a graduate of the University of Glamorgan, and possibly a little too obsessed with things that go bump in the night. Seriously, he has a Facebook page. You can look it up.

Jim's stories have appeared in *To Hull And Back Anthology 2016, Tales from the Boiler Room* and the soon-to-be-released *Eclectically Heroic Anthology.*

Twitter — @HorlockWarlock
Facebook

HOME AGAIN

By Adrian Ludens

They weren't even friends.

Adam didn't know why he'd agreed to ride along with Carson. Three hours of baking in a rust bucket with someone he barely knew had amounted to an interminable road trip indeed. But to hear Carson telling anyone who would listen—and even those who didn't—Adam and he were all but blood brothers.

"We've known each other almost our whole lives," Carson would invariably explain. "We grew up right across the street from each other!"

Adam wondered how Carson always managed to overlook the fact that he'd moved away at the end of First Grade. And Carson's family had left town a few years later. They'd reunited by happenstance in another city a decade later, and saw each other once or twice in passing, but Adam didn't think that qualified as knowing someone almost their whole life. Not that he was spiteful enough to call Carson on it. He'd concluded that the other man didn't have many friends.

Adam seldom returned to Springdale, though the town was often in his thoughts. He daydreamed about his grandparents and the farm he'd spent so much time exploring. He often wondered what had become of his classmates. He thought about the Frosty Treat, the old rodeo grounds on the edge of town, and the stand of trees behind his parents' trailer where he'd played with his diecast cars.

Carson brought up the idea of a road trip to their hometown via messages on Facebook. He badgered and bullied Adam until he finally relented, telling Carson he'd pay for half of the gas and buy dinner at Norm's Bar as long as Carson did all the driving.

They left at 7:00 A.M. on a Saturday and expected to arrive at noon.

And they weren't even friends.

Stop talking. Stop talking! STOP TALKING!

Carson didn't receive Adam's mental transmissions. Instead, he prattled on, reciting a constant litany of memories and anecdotes about Springdale. Any time Adam tried to introduce a new topic Carson ignored him.

"I remember riding our bikes over to the new water tower and having races around it. Did you ever race your bike around the water tower? Or were you too poor to have one? A bike, I mean." Carson turned his florid face toward Adam, as if eye contact would somehow help him hear clearly. "I'd always stop at Casey's for a Slushy on the way back. Remember Casey's? Had the plastic red sign made to look like bricks? It was right across from CR, the factory that went out of business. Did you ever—?"

"Yeah, yeah! Of course." Adam didn't even know what he had agreed with, but Carson guffawed and slapped the dash with one meaty hand.

"I figured! We coulda hung out more but you were too much of a mama's boy!"

Adam closed his eyes against the sun's glare shining furiously off the hood of Carson's old compact. He settled back, pretending to doze.

A pterodactyl screech of metal wiped all thought from Adam's brain and for a painful moment, it seemed as if his stomach and lungs had forcibly interchanged themselves within his body.

He jolted against his seat belt—

". . . awake?"

Adam took stock of himself and finding no apparent injuries heaved a sigh of relief. "What happened?"

"You were asleep, slacker." Carson punched his shoulder and then pointed a stubby finger at the windshield. "Look at that."

Carson had parked his car in front of a boxy two-story house. The exterior was a repulsive color Adam thought of as guacamole green. Weeds had overtaken the lawn. A gravel-scarred plastic Big Wheel sat on the driveway.

"My God! It looks just like I remember it." Carson threw open his car door and began to squirm from behind the wheel. "It hasn't changed at all!"

Adam grunted a vague assent and exited the vehicle. He gazed up at Carson's childhood home. Behind him, he knew, would be the Frosty Treat, now vacant and used for storage. He wanted to find the lot where he'd once lived in a mobile home with his folks, but for now his companion was dictating their actions. He shoved his hands in his pockets and shuffled along behind Carson, who bounded to the front door of his childhood dwelling with agility Adam hadn't expected.

"Door's open," Carson announced. He leaned into the darkness and called, "Hello? Anybody home?"

Adam stood back, enjoying the nostalgic smell of burning corncobs. He thought that practice had been outlawed in recent years, but realized people in small towns often did as they chose. A breeze caressed his skin as he watched an old man atop a riding mower navigate around a flowerbed in the yard next door. Man and machine wavered in the heat but Adam shivered for a reason he couldn't pinpoint.

He returned his attention to the stoop but his eyes found only a rectangle of darkness. Had Carson gone into the house? "Hey, Carson."

Though he hadn't shouted his companion's name Adam felt as if he had. Then he realized what had been bothering him, what had elicited the shiver.

No sound came from the riding mower. Adam checked the neighboring yard again. The old man and riding mower zigzagged over the grass—but silence reigned.

"Hey!"

Adam's whole body jerked like a marionette under a novice's control.

"Jesus! You scared the crap out of me," he muttered, trying to shake off his disquiet.

Carson had paled. "Come in here, slow poke. You gotta see this."

Adam looked around the interior. "Oh my lord. It's hideous."

Carson gave him a look. "Shut up! This is my parents' house."

"*Was* your parents' house, you mean?"

"No, look. The furniture, the paintings, the TV set—it's all the same!"

Adam scanned the room again. A black leather loveseat with yellow foam bursting from both cushions hunched in one corner like a giant beetle someone had stepped on. Paintings, one of a leopard and another of a gnarled tree in winter, hung on dark wood paneling. Small flowerpots hung from ceiling hooks in prisons of macramé. A woefully outdated television sat atop a rolling TV stand, sporting an old-fashioned rabbit-ears antenna and a bowtie of tinfoil.

"So your folks let whoever bought the house keep some of the stuff they didn't want."

Carson had moved to the foot of the stairs. He gripped the banister and gazed up at the second-story landing.

"I wouldn't go up there without asking the current owner first."

Carson didn't reply. He ascended the stairs two at a time.

"What the hell are you doing?" Adam called. "If someone calls the police—"

"I want to see my old room!" His stout companion's voice floated down the stairs from complete darkness. Adam half-expected to see the lingering grin of the Cheshire Cat.

He stood at the bottom of the flight of stairs frozen in indecision. The front door still stood open, inviting escape. This put him at ease. Had the door closed behind them, he felt sure claustrophobia would force him out onto the walk.

"It's still the same!" Carson called, exuberant. "Quit being such a pansy and get your ass up here! I have a Joe Montana rookie card—somewhere! And a complete set of Star Wars action figures!"

Intrigued, Adam followed Carson's voice up a creaking flight of narrow stairs. A dim light shone from a room halfway down the hall. The floorboards squeaked as Adam made his way to Carson's old room.

"It's all still here! I can't believe it!" Carson held something out to him. Adam took it and his breath caught in his throat.

"You had the blue Snaggletooth figure? This was a Sears exclusive or something wasn't it? This is worth a bunch of money now."

The toy felt greasy to the touch. Adam handed it back, wiped his fingers on his shirt, and gazed around the room. A poster of Daisy Duke hung on the closet door. Someone had oiled her skin to make it shimmer. Adam watched Carson pick up one figure after another, reliving memories.

Adam wandered over to a shelf. A trophy for a softball tournament stood nearest him. The faceplate read, "3rd Place, 1980 Summer Tourney." *From the days when you didn't get a trophy just for participating*, Adam thought. Movement caught his eye.

A square ant farm sat on the shelf next to the softball trophy. Adam leaned toward the wood-framed formicary, eyes narrowed. Living ants moved within.

Perplexed, Adam tried to collect his thoughts. What didn't make any sense was finding Carson's childhood possessions intact in a house he'd moved away from more than two decades prior. The ant farm might belong to the current occupant, in which case the living ants were normal.

He turned. "Dude, did you have an ant farm?"

"Huh?" Carson had been reaching under his bed for something when Adam spoke. "Yeah. Why?"

"Because it's still here. And the ants are still alive."

"You gotta be kidding me." Carson stood and stepped toward the shelf.

No, he'd been wrong. The ants had curled up and died long ago. Adam blinked and the ants returned to life, scurrying in their tunnels. Adam felt his chest tighten.

"They shouldn't be here." Carson's words stilled the ants again. In fact, the square glass walls and everything they contained faded from view.

Adam reached out but his fingers found only air. "What the hell?"

"It's like a hallucination or something," Carson said.

"I don't think your old toys should be here either." Adam gazed past his companion, who turned to look at his mattress. The action figures on it began to fade. So did the bed itself.

"Why'd you have to say that?" Carson moaned. "You ruined it for me!"

Adam didn't know what to say in response.

"I gotta . . ." Carson didn't finish. Instead, he turned and bolted from the room.

Adam followed a split second later. Carson had thundered to the end of the hall leading to the stairs at a full run. Adam opened his mouth to call out when Carson threw up his arms and dropped.

Adam gaped. His companion hadn't tumbled down the stairs. Instead, he'd simply plunged through the floor, as if he'd fallen through a hole. Adam felt a giddy wave of vertigo envelop him. He looked up, pinpointed the rope pull for the attic stairs and lunged for it.

As his hands clasped the rope, the entire floor dropped away beneath him. Adam pedaled his legs and hauled himself onto the attic steps. They were little more than wooden ladder slats. He looked down from his dizzying, isolated perch. Everything on the second level had collapsed onto the first, as if a garbage truck had purged its contents in the middle of a rummage sale. Adam squinted, searching for Carson. Had he survived the fall?

The attic ladder creaked and Adam scurried up into the relative safety of the structure's highest level. Here the wooden beams arched over him like the skeleton of a fossilized whale and faded away into the darkness. Except, he realized, it wasn't completely dark.

Something glowed at the far end of the room.

Orbs, like Christmas lights burning low, shone. Adam crept forward, giving his eyes time to adjust. He counted four large orbs and six smaller orbs. They looked like pairs of eyes. The idea froze his movement. He peered into the darkness. One pair of glowing orbs blinked, then another.

Adam made out their forms then. A cluster of figures, vaguely mammalian, huddled together in the high branches.

No, they couldn't be branches. Adam felt as if his perception had become fluid, ever changing. Even dream-like. A family of—what, exactly? Apes? Lemurs?—gazed at him, each with varying degrees of curiosity, suspicion, and alarm. Adam felt an icy serpent of fear coiling around his chest. *Don't think, just act!* This mental alarm overrode another, more dangerous, thought forming in his mind. Self-preservation instinct seized control.

Adam vaulted to the hole in the attic floor and swung from the ladder of steps. He summoned his memory of the nearest window. To his surprise, the window seemed closer than he'd expected. Pleased, Adam hurled himself toward the sill and caught onto the ledge with his arms. He scrambled against the floorless wall and lifted one leg and then the other until he balanced with his legs draped over the sill. He refused to acknowledge the jumbled rubble beneath him inside the house. Nor did he risk a glance at the attic—or forest canopy—for that's what it now seemed to resemble. He pushed the thought away.

You're just high, he told himself. *That has to be what's happening. Carson slipped you something in the car as a nasty joke and now you're having a bad trip, that's all. The house isn't melting and there aren't spectral monkeys. Now get back in the house before you fall and hurt yourself.*

Adam was about to follow his brain's advice when a blue pickup truck rounded the street corner, hopped the curb, and rolled to a stop below his perch. He stared at the new arrival in frank astonishment. From his precarious vantage point, Adam could see only part of the driver, but he saw enough that a wave of recognition and relief swept over him. The work-hardened hand holding the steering wheel was liver-spotted and gnarled but still looked like it could hoist a hay bale or carry a newborn calf. The blue and black flannel shirt covered a muscular arm that Adam knew would be 'farmer tan' white starting midway up the bicep. In the shadows of the cab, he could see blue jeans and the brim of a green cap emblazoned with the logo of a seed company. Adam could not see the face beneath the cap brim, but he knew it would be an amalgamation of John Wayne and Richard Nixon.

His grandfather had arrived just in time.

The pickup's bed was bursting with loose straw. The jarring groan of collapsing timbers thrust slivers of panic into Adam's spine. He pushed off and plummeted toward the truck, pinwheeling for a heart stopping moment before landing flat on his back in the straw. The pickup began to move, leaving the collapsing house behind them. Except the house was no longer collapsing; it wasn't there at all.

Mystified, Adam peered over the edge of the truck bed as his grandfather drove through town. He saw the mobile home he'd known as a child. Then he blinked and saw nothing but a vacant, weed-infested lot. Next came a row of storage units, but as Adam watched they faded and his favorite childhood haunt, the Frosty Treat, took its place. An older woman with hair piled high in a 60's beehive strolled out from the entrance.

Two blocks farther north a blue and white water tower loomed. Children scampered antlike around its base. As Adam watched, the tower faded. Instead, a covered wagon squeaked along rutted tracks, its driver holding the reins in one hand and mopping his brow with his free sleeve. Then, snow. White powder covered the landscape. Awestruck, Adam counted better than a dozen wooly mammoths laboring through the snow. They seemed unaware of the clan of fur-clad hunters awaiting them over the next ridge, stone-tipped spears at the ready.

Adam closed his eyes, overwhelmed. He felt weightless, neither hot nor cold. Despite his recent exertions, he didn't feel short of breath. Silence reigned. Adam kept still as a baby resting in the womb—or a cadaver decaying in a grave. An indeterminate amount of time passed.

A sudden cessation of motion caused him to roll forward in the truck's bed. Adam sat up and opened his eyes. Through the pickup's back window, he caught his grandfather's eyes in the rearview mirror. Deep creases but full of kindness and good humor surrounded them. Adam tried to speak but couldn't find the words.

His grandfather had driven him to the edge of town. He pointed his weathered left hand out the window at something on the road ahead. Adam stood for a better look.

Carson's nondescript car came into focus, tires exposed to the sky, two of them still spinning. Greasy smoke curled in tendrils from the engine block. A twisted shard of metal that Adam thought might be the hood lay in the opposite ditch.

Adam shuddered. The shudder became a convulsion. When the feeling had departed, the truck had as well.

Adam found himself kneeling in the middle of the road. His clothing hung from his arms and legs in tatters. The skin on his left thigh and arm looked like bloody raw hamburger. He tried to move his right arm and a clammy wave of nausea slapped him into submission. The ball of the joint appeared to be three or four inches farther forward than it should have been. Adam feared choking on the copper-flavored liquid that poured down his throat. With each labored breath sharp pain lanced through his ribs and into his lungs. He looked down to make sure one of the mammoth-hunters' spears wasn't lodged in his chest.

A hand ruffled his hair and then rested atop his head, like a priest offering a blessing. The pain diminished considerably. His grandfather's touch held him in stasis. Adam thought he understood the full significance of his grandfather's presence. It was, he realized, the same reason the house had appeared just as Carson remembered it.

The upturned wheels of the totaled car had only just stopped spinning. The curling smoke now billowed. The accident, Adam realized, had just happened. The tang of burnt rubber mixed with the thick acrid odor of burning oil. Everything that had just transpired in town had been . . . what, exactly?

Carson was, as far as he knew, still in town, buried beneath his belongings, or perhaps buried beneath his own memories, for even memories carried weight. He scanned the wreckage and his stomach lurched; a prone shape lay beneath a yellow tarp in the vehicle's shadow. Though a gust of wind rippled the edge of the cloth, the figure beneath it did not move. A measure of understanding came to him.

Adam realized that without his grandfather's arrival and intervention, he might have remained stranded back in town, in the impossible version of Springdale that existed only in his memory. All those layers, fading in and out of existence, as if all time existed in that one place. Each filmy layer fought for pre-eminence as the various former occupants remembered the area as it had been when they'd lived there.

Adam came to the realization and acceptance of it almost concurrently. His grandfather had died eight years prior. Yet here he stood, helping Adam find the inner strength to cope with the pain. No. That wasn't true; his grandfather somehow helped block the pain, staving it off until help arrived.

The keening wail of a siren came at last. Adam watched the ambulance approach, growing from a small white speck into a monolith that filled his entire field of vision. It circled, four-way lights flashing, and eased to a stop creating a protective barrier between him and oncoming traffic. His grandfather removed his hand and crackling bolts of agony surged through Adam's entire body, seemingly wanting to make up for lost time. He nearly blacked out as the paramedics hurried toward him.

"Sir, are you having trouble breathing?" The driver, a skinny guy with freckles, crouched beside him. Adam nodded. The man began efforts to curtail the bleeding while the other paramedic—a short woman who'd tied her black hair back in a no-nonsense ponytail—returned to the ambulance. Adam wondered what she would bring with her when she returned. Another question pressed itself into his thoughts: Where had his grandfather gone? He looked past the kneeling paramedic and found the old man.

He had relocated to a fenced-in field across the road from the accident. Beyond the fence posts and strands of barbed wire, a herd of Holstein cattle grazed. Adam's grandfather had been a dairy farmer for most of his life. The black and white cattle seemed to sense the ghostly figure, but instead of stampeding away, they began ambling toward him.

The female paramedic returned carrying what appeared to be a big plastic neck brace. She also had something that looked like it might be for his shoulder.

". . . pain in your chest?"

Adam realized he had missed most of the red-haired paramedic's question but got the gist of it. He used his bleeding left arm to point out two separate parts of his rib cage. The man nodded.

"There's a good chance you have internal bleeding. We're going to immobilize your neck as a precaution and get you onto a stretcher as quickly as possible. Then we'll drive to the Emergency entrance at Dayton County Hospital. Springdale's clinic doesn't have the equipment needed."

Adam watched the cattle milling around his grandfather, surrounding him. He appeared to scratch the head of one and pat the flank of another. The cattle lowed. Adam found the sound soothing. He closed his eyes, and considered the countless acts of kindness he'd received from his grandfather over the years. He treasured the silly stories, the hayrides, Slinky races down the basement steps, and the butterscotch candies secretly bestowed before supper like contraband. As a child, he'd never stopped to appreciate all the meals freely given, never considered the sacrifices made to ensure he received birthday and Christmas gifts, even in the leanest of years. Naiveté had permitted him to accept these blessings as a matter of course. Why had he never thought to thank the old man?

Adam opened his eyes and propped himself up with his elbows.

His grandfather had vanished. Only the cattle remained. Adam strained and squinted, hoping for one more glimpse of the kindly old man.

The woman spoke. "Take it easy; once we get you stabilized, we can be in Dayton less than thirty minutes. You'll make a full recovery, I promise."

Fresh tears pricked his eyes and spilled down Adam's cheeks. He'd missed his chance. His grandfather had interceded on his behalf and brought him back from the brink. With his fate no longer in question, the spectral image had dissolved from view.

"I'm not dying today." Adam took a ragged breath and smiled, exposing blood-smeared teeth. "When my time does come, though, I hope I can find my way back here."

He saw the paramedics exchange a mystified glance as they secured him to the stretcher. They lifted him then, and Adam felt a brief sensation of weightlessness. He fluttered a hand in the direction of the lingering cattle.

"I need to come back, thank him face to face. I owe him at least that much."

Adrian Ludens is the author of *Ant Farm Necropolis* (A Murder of Storytellers LLC), and is a member of the Horror Writers Association with Active status. Recent and favorite publication appearances include *DOA 3* (Blood Bound Books), *HWA Poetry Showcase IV*, *Blood in the Rain 3* (Cwtch Press) and *Zippered Flesh 3* (Smart Rhino Publications). Adrian is a radio announcer and a fan of hockey, reading and writing horror fiction, swimming, and exploring abandoned buildings. Visit him at http://www.adrianludens.com.

JENNIFER BRINGS IT TO WORK

By Jack Lothian

Monday

Jennifer brings it to work. She is twenty minutes late and has missed the morning meeting, a meeting at which our manager shared his concerns over the sales report we're due to deliver to head office at the end of the week. The word 'downsizing' was used along with 'redundancies.' He encouraged us to make a final push in these remaining days, to try and turn things around before it's too late. He is tired and the circles beneath his eyes tell of late nights crunching figures, juggling numbers, trying to find a safe passage through this oncoming financial storm.

Some of us have families. Debts. Mortgages. And even though we work for a company that sells health insurance, many of us don't have comprehensive coverage of our own. We've been waiting for a miracle, some upturn in fortunes, but the cold reality of the situation is upon us. We are scared of the future.

Yet the moment Jennifer walks in, cradling it in her arms, all this is forgotten.

I am on a sales call when she enters. It was clear within the first few minutes of conversation that the man on the other end of the line has no intention to purchase any of our health care packages but policy dictates that I have to follow through the script of questions, laminated and pinned on my cubicle wall, beat by beat, until the call reaches an end.

Yet when I see Jennifer coming down the aisle, heading for her desk, carrying it, I find myself rising up, removing my head-set, not even bothering to finish the sales talk. I'm drawn to her, to it. There is no decision, no choice. All around the office my co-workers are doing the same thing, standing up from cubicles, moving towards Jennifer, as if on some pre-arranged signal.

We gather round her, looking at it, in various states of awe. It is beautiful. Miriam from accounts tentatively asks if she can hold it. Jennifer nods kindly. Of course she can. She places it in Miriam's arms. Miriam stands there, staring down at it, her breathing shallow, her eyes like little dark pools of water.

"Oh my," she says. "It really is wonderful."

We ask Jennifer where it came from. Jennifer says she found it lying on her door step that morning. I feel a twinge of jealousy, that she could have a life where such things happen, that while I was forcing myself into the shower, bleary eyed and alone, she was opening her door to such a sight. I want to say something cutting, to try and puncture her joy, bring her back down to where the rest of us are, but then I find myself looking at it, and I feel a sense of wonder rushing over me, washing away any jagged thoughts.

The manager comes over to tell us to get back to work, but when he sees it he stops mid-stride.

"What is that . . .?" he asks.

Jennifer just gives him a gentle smile. He keeps staring at it, frowning a little. "I'm not sure you can bring that to work."

Jennifer gazes down at it. "No," she says, and although her voice is quiet, I can sense the edge underneath. "I can bring it to work."

Its face is peering out from the grey blankets she has swaddled it in, and she strokes its cheek, almost absentmindedly. The manager stands there, nodding for a moment, as if he accepts that, but I can feel the unease reverberating off him.

"Would you like to hold it?" Jennifer says, offering the bundle to him.

He shakes his head. He walks back through the bullpens and cubicles, reminding us that we have sales targets to reach, that the end of the week isn't far away. He is trying to sound authoritative, in control, but he stumbles over his words. He walks into his office, never looking back, closing the door behind him. The blinds are already down. I hear the faint click of the lock. I want to watch for a moment, to see if he'll peer out through the slats but already I am turning back, drawn to look at it once again.

I know I should get back to work. The manager is right—we only have until Friday. Our livelihoods hang in the balance. I should be sitting at my terminal, making calls from the list, chasing sales, but I already know that won't be happening.

We won't get much work done today. Nobody is concerned by this, as we stand there, a small crowd around Jennifer.

We are lucky. We are blessed.

Tuesday

In the dream I am in a maze of cubicles that stretch out forever. Strip lights flutter overhead. Monitors flicker an uneasy green glow but they cannot penetrate the darkness here that seems thick and heavy. I can barely see in front of my face.

This is our office but it is also somewhere else at the same time, somewhere oddly familiar, and the fact I seem to have been here before terrifies me in a way I can't explain.

Then I hear it calling to me from across the room, somewhere buried in the bullpens and workspaces. I try to run towards its cry, but the ground is sludge beneath my feet and my muscles feel like rotting candy-floss. I look up and realize I was never in the office after all. I am standing on a shore. Dark water laps at my feet. I get the sense that I have been standing here for a long time. Maybe forever.

The tide is coming in and out so quickly, so violently, that it leaves a gulf behind it, a muddy seabed where scores of silver fish gasp and thrash, before the water crashes back in, sweeping them up. Over and over again. In the distant surf giant black shapes rise and fall beneath the sea. The sky is alight with stars.

It is still calling me, but now it is joined by other voices, first one, then many, a cacophony howling in some language I don't understand. Louder and louder as those black shapes burst through the water, towering overhead, and just as they fall upon me I, of course, wake up.

I lie in the half-light, listening to early morning traffic outside. I try not to imagine where Tony is now. What he is doing. Who he is with. I'm forty-five years old. It's too late to start over. I can feel all that time trailing behind me, out of reach, gone forever. A quiet panic starts to build and threatens to overwhelm me and I sit up in bed, unable to catch my breath for a moment, shaken. I consider calling in sick, but then I remember Friday's deadline and as bad as things might feel right now, they could become a lot worse.

I am running late and by the time I reach the office there is already a crowd around Jennifer's cubicle. Even though my view is obscured I know instantly that she has brought it into work again. I can feel its presence in the room, a shift in the atmosphere, in the humidity.

The manager intercepts me before I can join them. He lightly takes my arm, guiding me towards his office. I shake my head, trying to keep moving towards Jennifer's bullpen.

"It'll just be a minute," he says. "Please."

He closes the door behind him as we enter his office. He offers me a seat but I don't respond so he awkwardly perches at the end of his desk instead as some sort of compromise. He smiles at me, like he hopes I will initiate the conversation but I just look towards the blinds, knowing that beyond them, out there in the office, the others are gazing down at it.

"I think this might be a problem," he says.

I still don't speak. I can feel the fast beat of my heart. I want to leave his office and go back out there. This isn't fair. It is a cruelty to keep me away from it, in here.

"Do you think it's a problem?" he says and his tone suggests that he'd really like me to answer.

I shake my head. This isn't a problem. No.

"Nobody did any work yesterday."

He approaches me, cautious, like I'm a feral creature that might bolt at any moment. "We've got a long way to go if we're going to hit those sales targets by the end of the week. And well, for God's sakes . . . look at it."

He walks towards the window and opens the blinds. I feel a wave of relief at seeing them all gathered round Jennifer out there. It is still here. "This isn't normal," he says, and his voice cracks a little. "We have to do something. We have to talk to them."

"Why?"

My question seems to confuse him and his mouth moves before he can fully find the words. "Something is wrong here. It's like when you have a dream and you try to remember what happened but the details keep slipping away and . . . I'm not sure I even remember why I brought you in here, in the first place." He shakes his head, his hand to his mouth. "Doesn't that seem strange? Do you remember us walking in here? Do you?"

After the accident, when I was still in the hospital, he was the first one from the office to pay a visit. He brought some flowers, because he didn't know what else to bring in a situation like that. He didn't ask many questions, he didn't even ask how I was feeling and I was grateful for that at least.

I see the worry etched on his face, feel his desperation, and I find myself nodding, trying to remember why I didn't continue my work yesterday, why I walked away from a call in progress, but then I see movement from the corner of my eye and look back out to the office, and Miriam has stepped to the side a little and I have a clear line of sight and I can feel it, looking at me, and for one glorious moment nothing else exists outside of this.

I open the door and my manager tries to say something but I am already moving across the room, weightless, on air, drifting towards the rest of them as they congregate around Jennifer's cubicle.

Jennifer sees me and smiles and I smile back at her. Miriam is muttering something to me and it takes me a moment to hear her properly, as she tries to tell me about a dream she had last night, a black beach, dark water, how the stars overhead seemed altered in a way that terrified her. She says something about an eye opening, mentions the word leviathan, possibly as an adjective, maybe as a noun but I have stopped listening long before she breaks down into whispered sobs. I just want to savor this moment, standing here with my co-workers, in the warm glow of its presence.

Phones ring unanswered. Emails stack up unread. We stay exactly where we are and where we are meant to be.

This is Tuesday in the office.

Wednesday

I do not remember going to sleep or waking, or what my dreams were made of. I open my eyes and find myself standing before the sink, toothbrush in hand, the faucet running, unfamiliar words jangling in my head.

After the accident Tony would often find me standing here in the mornings, similarly unable to recall how long I'd been here. Maybe minutes. Maybe hours. I was sleepwalking a lot at the time. He would guide me back to bed, whisper reassuring words, telling me this was something that would be pass.

It didn't pass though and in time his understanding turned to resentment. He wanted me to let go, but I couldn't. I wanted to cling onto my grief, to wrap my arms around it, to let it thrash and throw me around.

Then the incident at the supermarket happened and everything seemed to change between us for good. They had it all wrong. I wasn't taking the baby anywhere. All I did was pick her up from her pram, walk with her for a few minutes along the aisles. I just wanted to know what it felt like, to glimpse a life that should have been mine. They could have given me one more minute.

That's all I wanted. To be happy, truly happy, for just a moment or so.

It wasn't that much to ask.

The manager is waiting for Jennifer when she arrives. We have all been watching the door, expectant. Miriam brings up the sales report, but it is a half-hearted attempt to focus on work and none of us respond. Then Jennifer comes in and the office seems a little bit brighter, a little more real. Of course, she has brought it back with her once more.

The manager places his hand on her arm though, moving her to his office. We are all risen, craning to look. Jennifer is trying to say something to him, but he is talking over her. Their voices are indistinct. We start to move forward, closer, but they have reached his office already and he ushers her inside, closing the door, locking it.

The blinds are down. They are sealed away from us.

We try to get on with our work. We look at sales figures, data, leads. We make the right moves with our fingers on keyboards and the right noises with our voices on the phone. But we are not here. We are inside that office with them.

Lunch time comes. Nobody heads out to eat or even orders in. Our vigil is all that matters now. Sometimes we see a shadow beyond the blinds, somebody moving in the office, and a murmur of anticipation ripples across the room. But the office door remains locked and closed.

Outside, cars pass down the street. Commuters walk, eyes fixed on cellphones, blind to the world around them. Trains rattle underground. The sun sinks down, turning the sky orange and then red and finally an unsure shade of black. Lights flicker on across the city, a blanket of stars.

We are all still here. The phones don't ring anymore. There is no sound of typing, of printers smoothly ejecting documents. We barely breathe. All the lights are off, except for the manager's office. It is aglow at the end of the room like a faraway city that we can never visit, that will forever be glimpsed in the distance, out of reach.

Then we hear the lock turning. Our glazed eyes switch back into focus. The manager leans his head out. He sees our darkened outlines, staring back at him.

He tells us to go home for the night.

He closes the office door again. The lock turns. The light goes off.

We go home.

Thursday

The door to the manager's office is still closed and locked. The blinds remain down, the light is off inside. Yet overnight we have made a silent, unacknowledged decision to get back to work. We have a sense of purpose now. We have our leads.

The automated system patches us through to people around the country and we tell them how tremendous our medical insurance policy is and how much money they can save by switching providers.

We outline the terrible things that could befall their family without our service. We follow the scripts pinned up in our bullpens, next to photos of families, friends, colleagues, signs that say you don't have to be mad to work here, schedules, calendars, lunch menus. We tell our customers about successful claims that have been paid out before, about special rates on ambulatory and hospital care, and our fast, free, no obligation quotes. We also make sure to tell them about the negative spaces that exist between letters, the hidden provinces concealed by words, how language evolved to control us so we could no longer see the invisible kingdom that lies beyond the veil. We are removing these verbal blindfolds, these constraints, speaking in a tongue that none of us understand or remember, but have always known, buried somewhere in our primal past, as man stood naked under the cosmos and stared up into the eternal.

We are chanting, discordant consonants collapsing into unknowable vowels. I can see Miriam crying into her headset as her mouth makes strange shapes and the sound pours from her throat in an unending torrent. Her nails dig into her palms, thin slivers of blood trickling onto white sleeves.

I smile at her and she smiles back, helpless, her mouth still moving, like she is merely a grinning puppet. The man on the other end of my phone-line is shouting in my ear now, his words running into each other; they are the sounds of an ancient tomb opening, they are the sounds of a dead moon falling from the sky, they are the sounds that are coming from every mouth in the room, through every tinny headset, across telephone lines, across electronic signals, across radio waves, spreading and spreading and spreading, like waves onto a dark shore, like a herald for what is to come.

We keep going all day and all night. We do not stop. We are good workers.

Friday

Today we have to deliver the sales report to head office.

The streets are deserted. Headless streetlamps sparkle in the morning air. Smoke drifts from subway entrances. A black sun shines overhead.

Friday is the best day.

The carpet in the office is thick and sticky. Miriam is slumped over her terminal, bent forwards as if to prostrate before some inevitable god. Her jaw hangs open, still moving, still trying to form words and sounds, despite the fact it is swollen and dislocated. Her hands are raised a little, opening and closing, gently clutching at the air. She reminds me of a scuttled crab.

Jennifer sits in the cubicle next to mine. I have not seen her since the manager led her into the office on Wednesday. Her skin is ashen and she has lost weight. She quietly tells me that all this is a dream, but just not our dream. She tells me not to be sad. Nothing can end that truly did not exist. I remind her that the sales report is due. It is very important for reasons I can't seem to remember. Something about downsizing, although the concept of size seems vaguely ridiculous now.

Nevertheless, I sit down and start to collate the figures for the month. Expenses. Sales. Growth. Profit. Loss. My fingers tap lightly on the keyboard and I can see my reflection on the terminal screen, dim and distant, a ghost.

"What was it, Jennifer?" I ask as I insert the numbers into a spreadsheet. "What was it you found on your doorstep?"

"You don't remember . . .?"

"I keep forgetting things. Did we all go on a work outing somewhere? For some reason I remember a beach. Sand. Maybe it was night." I am about to say something more but even that drifts away. Compiling the report should be Miriam's job but she is no longer moving, crouched at her desk, a husk.

"You don't remember," Jennifer repeats, no longer a question.

"Do you?"

She shakes her head. "I remember it was a Monday. I remember the alarm on my phone waking me up. Showering. Doing my hair, my make-up, getting dressed. I was hurrying because I was worried I was going to be late and I'd been late quite a few times this past month." She stops for a moment, shivering. "I remember opening the door and stepping out and looking down and there it was and . . ."

"What was it?" I ask again, even though I both know and don't know the answer to that at the same time, and maybe what she saw isn't what I saw, or what Miriam saw. Maybe we all saw what we needed to see.

Jennifer shrugs, smiles helplessly. "I just knew I should bring it to work. That I should show everyone."

She falls silent, staring off into some distant place. Her hands are black and charred. I finish the sales reports and email it. The document makes a satisfying whooshing sound as it is sent and I imagine a little paper airplane, taking off into the air, weaving between the buildings and bridges of this town, flying out above the highways, towards head office.

I get up and walk down the aisle to the manager's office. I knock lightly on the door and enter. He is sitting behind his desk. He has been crying. I tell him I have sent the sales report to head office.

He tells me it is quite possible that head office no longer exists. He is shaking and he struggles to get the words out. I walk over and put my arms around his head, pulling him close, like a mother to a child.

I tell him I am glad that Jennifer did what she did. I can't imagine how my life would have gone on otherwise. I can't even remember all those feelings that used to hang over me like a heavy cloak. There was a lonely room. A shattered heart. An empty space. A multitude of disappointments and regrets, nurtured and tended, so they would never fade. They seem so small and insignificant now that I find it hard to believe they even registered at the time.

I stand there in the manager's office, looking beyond him, to the stars blinking into darkness, the endless universe above, the black ocean below. There is a cold wind blowing in from places we could never even dream of and a whole new world waiting to engulf our own.

There are tears in my eyes and I am smiling, for my heart is finally full and I am so grateful for this gift.

I am so grateful Jennifer brought it to work.

Jack Lothian works as a screenwriter for film and television and is currently show runner on the forthcoming HBO/Cinemax series *Strike Back*. His short fiction has appeared in Helios Magazine Quarterly, Parsec Ink's *Triangulation : Appetites*, Omnestream Entertainment's *Out of Frame* and *Down With The Fallen* from Franklin/Kerr Press.

THE ENAMELLED CROWN

By Steve Toase

Seline sheltered in her bedroom and ran her tongue across the back of her teeth. Uneven and discoloured enamel tasted bitter. She reached down the side of the bed for a bag of sweets, unwrapped the first one and let it settle in the cup of her palm. With her other hand she smoothed the glittering crimson wrapper against the bedspread.

Just the one, to take the taste away, she said to herself, holding the toffee in the gap between jaw and cheek. Rich butter syrup melted against her gums. The flavour of plaque did not go, just swam in sugar that sweetened her throat for a moment, then was gone.

Her hand was back in the bag and unwrapping the second before the flavour of the first had faded. She held it in her fingers, letting it tack to her skin before placing it in her mouth.

"Where have you been hiding them?"

Her father shadowed the door, arms folded like a bird clasping its wings.

"I didn't hide them," Seline lied, sliding two unwrapped sweets out of the bag and up her sleeve. Hoped the light leaking around her father did not shimmer the foil.

"I went through this room and took out all the packets I could find. How did I miss that one?"

Seline shrugged, not wanting to give away any more clues, and tried to push two more into the gap between mattress and bedframe.

"And today of all days."

"We have to go in," her father said. They stood on the pavement, not even making it into the small, untended yard. From outside there was little to distinguish the dentist's surgery from the homes in the rest of the terrace. Just a peeling sign proclaiming names and qualifications of those working, and heavy metal shutters to keep out those looking for free lidocaine. His fingers dug into her shoulder and before Seline could protest, they were up the path, the doorbell rung, and inside the building.

The dentist waiting room still had the cornicing and fireplace, now unused, from when it was the family lounge. In the corner, an aquarium stood on an old chest of drawers of yellowed and peeling pine. Goldfish and black mollies swarmed frilled weeds that rose and fell against the rhythmic water pump's current. Seline's father held out a magazine for her. She ignored it and went back to watching the fish chase each other, their scales paled by the fluorescent lights in the lid. Covering her hand with her sleeve Seline unwrapped the humbug, faked a cough and slid it into her mouth. With her fingernails she tapped the glass. The gilled spatters of colour streaked to the gravel and hid inside the plastic castle.

"They do have teeth."

The dental nurse stood beside her, most of her pristine white uniform hidden behind a plastic apron spattered with liquids Seline did not recognise.

"Their teeth are at the back of their throats," she continued, pointing a manicured nail past her own veneered and straightened incisors.

"They just fall out and then grow back. Imagine that. No need for us then." She smiled, turning to Seline's father who laughed as if they shared a private joke. "The dentist is seeing both of you today? Correct?"

Seline's father nodded and stood up.

"Please, this way." She held the door open, waiting while Seline's father gathered their coats and gloves. Hand over her face, Seline crunched the mint to splinters and swallowed.

The surgery was in what was once the front bedroom, and smelt of deep cleaning and spit. Every surface polished to hygiene, the room spotless and pristine. The dentist was not. He hunched over the worktop, dressed in beige trousers and an old Argyll knit jumper, as if all the nicotine and faded colours of the wallpaper that once decorated the room had seeped into him. His hair was thinned and clothes tattered as if they couldn't quite contain him. Noticing he wasn't alone, he reached up to a peg and unhooked a white coat. Slid his arms inside. Seline watched his hands shake, until he noticed her looking.

"Nurse, please get the first patient settled," he said. He paused and stared at Seline with watery eyes. "I'll see the girl first," he said, and turned back to what he was doing.

"Yes, Mr. Fortnum."

The counter was covered in plaster-casts of teeth. Seline watched him trace a finger over the crowns and incisors, small plumes of white dust coming away on his skin.

"This way please," the nurse said, ushering Seline away from her father toward the plastic-coated chair at the centre of the room. Against the far wall of the surgery was a second aquarium, this one murky, the water heavy with rotting vegetation. A yellowed fish swam out of the gloom and attached its mouth to the glass, a circle of razor sharp teeth gnawing away at the streaks of dirt.

"Seline, is it?" Mr. Fortnum said, handing a folder of notes to the nurse, who smiled and tucked them into the bottom level of the trolley. "Been a while since your last check up."

"I try to get her to do the right thing. Sometimes I think she has it in her head that if these drop out more will grow back, but that doesn't happen with your second set," her father said, his words tripping over themselves. "Once they're gone, they're gone."

"Exactly," the nurse said. "You're not a fish."

Out of the corner of her eye Seline saw her father look confused and take a deep breath as he always did when making a point.

"I keep telling her that she needs to look after them now, while it's free. Won't get second chances later. She doesn't listen."

"Children rarely do," Mr. Fortnum said. His voice was slow and considered, and as he settled Seline's head into a better position she flinched away from his hand against her neck.

The chair tipped back, the light above came on. An electric sunburst robbed Seline of all sight apart from her peripheral vision.

She felt fingers in her mouth, the counting of her teeth a liturgy between the dentist and his nurse. Even through the gloves his hands felt rough against her cheeks, the coloured vinyl hiding some infection that plated his skin. His tremor returned. The probe twitched against her gum, and Seline flinched.

"Ow," she tried to say, but the word could not find a way past the grip against her cheek.

"Sorry," the nurse said. Mr. Fortnum stayed silent.

"Vacuum please," Mr. Fortnum said, and Seline felt the tube slide into her mouth.

He moved around to stand beside her head, her face resting against the cotton of his white coat. The grinding sound reminded Seline of the noise her father made when he was asleep and bills were due. Anxiety chipping away his own enamel. This rasping was muffled. Close. She glanced up at Mr. Fortnum, then the nurse. Both wore masks obscuring their mouths as if the rot in Seline's teeth might climb out and infect them. The sound was closer.

Mr. Fortnum reached over her while the nurse passed him a small mirror. The noise intensified, grinding away at nothing, then fell back as he began examining her teeth once more.

Above her head the intense light tilted away. Underneath Seline the chair pitched her up into a sitting position. Across the room the fish still gnawed at streaks of algae. Maybe the grating noise was the creature trying to chew an escape through the plated glass.

Mr. Fortnum pulled across a stool and sat in front of Seline, masking her father from sight. Hand still twitching, he reached into his pocket for a pair of smudged glasses, slid them in place and yawned. At the back of his throat she saw a flash of something bone white, then his mouth shut and it was gone. Seline glanced over at the fish-tank. The suckermouth had dropped back into the murk, hidden and out of sight.

"There is good news and bad," he said, leaning forward. His breath smelt too clean and she tried to shift back in her seat.

"The bad news is that your teeth are in terrible condition. Terrible. There's no point in sugar-coating it." Behind him her father laughed too loud. "But you're setting yourself down a very bad road." He leaned back, wincing as he did so as if something sharp caught in his stomach. "Nurse, please can you pass me today's extractions."

"Of course, Mr. Fortnum," the nurse said, passing over a tray crammed with bloody and yellowed teeth.

He took off his white coat and gripped the proffered metal.

"These are from an appointment I had this morning. A boy not much older than you. Liked his sweets too. His breath also had the reek of humbugs and toffees like yours." He picked up a molar and turned it around, the light above Seline's head reflected off the stained enamel. She watched him run his nail across the blackened edge of a cavity, scraping off a shudder of plaque.

"We had to extract seven of his teeth. That's it. Gone. No more."

Seline tried to listen to the words. All her focus was on the way he held the tooth, turning it one way or another like a jeweller assessing the clarity of some rare diamond.

"She just stashes the sweets around her room. Hides them under her pillow, and down the side of her bed. Don't know where she gets the money from. I don't buy them for her."

Seline started to speak, and out of the corner of her eye was sure that Mr. Fortnum lifted the molar to his own mouth, swallowing it down.

Turning quickly to the tray she tried counting the still bloodied teeth lying on the stainless meta. They must have been jarred around and lay in a confusion making them impossible to number. Instead, she looked back at Mr. Fortnum. He sat as still as before, now holding a rotten incisor up to her. At the corner of his mouth she thought she saw a spatter of dried blood. His tongue flicked out and it was gone.

"They used to tell children, my father told me, that if I left decayed teeth for the tooth fairy, then the tooth fairy would empty my jaws. To make up for the short fall."

Seline struggled to see Mr. Fortnum as ever having parents.

"Do children believe in the tooth fairy these days?" he continued.

"I'm not sure what she believes in these days," her father said. The nurse smiled and shrugged, an unspoken understanding passing between them.

"Oh, it's good to believe," Mr. Fortnum said, reaching out and opening Seline's mouth again. "Helps keep us on the straight and narrow. Just how I like teeth." There was a pause before the nurse laughed, and even then it scratched out like a failing soundtrack. Seline avoided his wet gaze and stared at his stomach. Underneath the brown wool something undulated, rippling from one side to the other. To distract herself she glanced back at the aquarium. Deep in the undergrowth she saw a flash of gold. A streak of red plumed up through the grey water.

"I'm going to send you off to the hygienist's room for my nurse to scrape your teeth. Get them clean. Pleasant. A good descale and polish. We might be able to slow some of the damage."

Seline slid off the chair, the floor meeting her feet too soon. The nurse took her arm and led her toward the door. On the chair in the corner her father struggled to collect their outside clothes and follow.

"If you wouldn't mind stopping here, Mr. Drayman, we can do your check-up, and sort out the finer details of Seline's treatment."

Seline paused at the door, resisting the nurse's encouragement and waited for her father to follow.

"I'll meet you downstairs," he said, turning to take the official looking papers Mr. Fortnum held out. Seeing Seline staring, the dentist smiled, the corners of his mouth a little too far back. The grin a little too crowded.

"Come with me. We have other jobs to do." The nurse pulled her out of the surgery room and back out onto the landing.

The hygienist's treatment room was smaller, dirtier and crammed into what had been the attic. Once the nurse had Seline laid in the chair, various attachments scraped away the traces of poor care. Over the rotations of metal against her teeth Seline heard creaking from below.

"Just the building contracting in the heat," the nurse said by way of explanation. "Spit."

Jaw aching, Seline stood and waited for the nurse to follow her. She looked up as if only just noticing her patient again.

"You'll have to find your own way out. I have to clean up here. Cleanliness is next to godliness," she said, shutting her out.

Groping along the wall, Seline found the light switch, and stared at the faded carpet under her feet. No-one had bothered about hygiene outside the shine of the surgery. For a moment she stood on the top step, unsure what to do. Where to go. Whether to go at all. No-one to guide her back through the building. She held the bannister and pulled herself down through the house.

On the next floor the main surgery was off to one side, the door slightly open. Through the gap she saw Mr. Fortnum standing in the middle of the room, his shirt off. From a collection of surgical tools, he picked up a scalpel and made an incision in his chest. She watched him hold the tray he flourished earlier, more teeth than she remembered. He pressed one after the other into the pocket of flesh. Somewhere inside him Seline heard each one clatter into place. The enamelled crowns stretched his skin tight. Inside the gaping wound she watched still bloody roots of extracted teeth knit into his exposed ribs, severed nerves curling around the curved surface of the bone. In several places across his chest the sharp edges started to lacerate their way through. Tiny petals of blood streaked down to stain the waist of his trousers.

"You shouldn't be loitering here. Your father will be wondering where you are."

Seline turned to face the nurse as the older woman's hand slammed the surgery door shut, then gripped Seline's arm tight. "And this house is so old and so full of hazards we wouldn't want you to come to harm."

In the waiting room her Dad sat in the corner by the aquarium, slight streaks on his chin.

"Are you okay?" Seline said, wriggling away from the nurse's grip.

He smiled, the gaps in-between the remaining teeth still raw and bloody.

"He said they were far too gone to save, rotted through. I only want to make sure you don't have to go through the same as me," his words slurred into each other.

"Remember," said the nurse, opening her own mouth wide until Seline could barely see her eyes. "They don't grow back."

Seline stared, transfixed at the slight flash of white near the back of the woman's throat, until a clatter in the corner of the room distracted her. A golden scaled fish smashed itself into the glass of the aquarium again and again.

Steve Toase currently lives in Munich, Germany.
His fiction has appeared in *Aurealis, Not One Of Us,* and *Cafe Irreal* amongst others. In 2014, "Call Out" (first published in *Innsmouth Magazine*) was reprinted in *The Best Horror Of The Year 6,* and his story "Fate's Mask" was mentioned in the summation. His story "Not All The Coal That Is Dug Warms The World" was included in Ellen Datlow's Honourable Mentions Longlist for *Best Horror of the Year 8,* and has just been featured on the *Tales To Terrify* podcast. He also writes regularly for *Fortean Times.*

Recently, he worked with Becky Cherriman and Imove on *Haunt,* about Harrogate's haunting presence in the lives of people experiencing homelessness in the town.

www.stevetoase.wordpress.com
www.facebook.com/stevetoase1
@stevetoase

To get free flash fiction to your inbox Tinyletter.com/stevetoase

REFLECTED IN THE EYES OF WOLVES

By Joachim Heijndermans

As a boy of ten, Jack laughed. He laughed along with the other boys and girls of his age. Oh, the fun they had from their place at the window, seeing the wolves come in their packs, rushing past their houses. Their great teeth gleaming in the moon's light, eyes bright with hunger. That elegant way they ran. Dancers of gray and white, gaining on the old farts whose bones creaked with each step. Beautiful hunters of the night, picking up the scent of their prey and claiming their prize.

Oh, how they laughed when they saw the elderly try to run. Run away from their certain doom. Run away from the teeth and claws that would rip them to shreds. Their arms flailing and that hilarious wobbling motion they made with each hurried step, which reminded Jack of scarecrows flailing in the wind. The children shrieked with joy when one of the geriatrics would trip and be shredded to pieces within seconds by the hungry pack. They would be so disappointed when one of them got away, but that rarely happened these days. No one would come to help those geezers. Not when the wolves hunted. What a sight! What a thrill. A fantastic show for everyone of all ages.

Well, all ages up until sixty that is. That's when you just might become the prey. That's when the wolves begin eyeing you up and hunt you down in the streets. And no one would do a damn thing to help you. That's the way things were. That's why the wolves were brought back. The packs need to eat. The herd, that is us, needed to be thinned. Executive decision. It's humane. It's fair. It's necessary.

And like all the other children, Jack laughed when it happened. It was a show. A happening. No game or movie could beat the sight of a pack of powerful animals ripping their prey to shreds. The funniest part would be whenever the catch of the day tried to beg for help. Didn't they know by now? There wasn't anyone coming for them. What would be the point? You can't stop the wolves once they were on the prowl. No one would ever even try.

As a boy of fifteen, Jack asked. The question most children asked at that age.

“Why do we let the wolves hunt? Why do we let them kill and eat up all the old folks?”

His brother punched him on the arm and told him not to ask stupid questions. His mother sent him to his room without dinner. His teacher made him stay after school. Only his father was kind enough to answer, if you considered sharing the truth a kindness.

"You see, kiddo, the wolves are there to save us. They're here to protect us from ourselves, so we don't starve by wasting our dwindling supplies when feeding the leeches of society. There's too many of us, you see. Too many people who eat and use up all the things that we need to keep things running. We can't allow parasites to thrive while we, the healthy and the strong, work and struggle. But the laws forbid us from harming each other in any way. So, with no other options, the Party looked to our enemies from the past from back when we weren't on top of the food chain. We turned to our old enemies from within the forest. The wolves.

"Back when we were savages, these great beasts could only be stopped by our weapons and our fire. We drove them back until there weren't any left. But stopping them led to no-one dying outside of old age. No-one dying led to too many of us. Too many led to conflict over space and food. War. Hunger. Disease. We nearly wiped ourselves out, you see. That's when the new order decreed to have the wolves brought back.

"The wolves became our wardens, culling the old geezers, the fatties, the druggies and the retards. We let them hunt so we will never destroy ourselves ever again. And that is the last we'll ever speak of this. Now go help your mom set the table."

Jack accepted this. If his father said it was for the greater good, then it must be true. He wouldn't lie. Not to his son. And now that he knew the reasons behind the hunt were just, he could laugh again with the other children, as they watched the packs hunt the streets for society's vermin.

Oh, how he laughed when he saw an old man running down the street from his bedroom window. The pack of wolves that stalked and surrounded him, cutting off his way to home. He gasped when the man tried to fight the hunters off with his walking cane. He cheered when a gray female pounced at him and ripped his throat apart. The blood ran through the gutters as the pack ripped their prey apart. What a sight! What a hunt.

"Beautiful," he gasped.

As young man of twenty, Jack witnessed. He witnessed the violence that was unleashed on insurgents who opposed the law. He saw the price of resistance firsthand and how the law deals with those who would deny the wolves their hunting rights.

It was another young man, about roughly his age, with broad shoulders and blue eyes. He attended the university as well, albeit in a different class. Jack talked with him on occasion. He seemed like a sensible fellow. A quiet young man who would never dream of being insurgent. Thus, all the greater Jack's surprise when he witnessed the young man do the unthinkable.

It was near dark. A pack of six surrounded an elderly woman. They had her cornered. The crone pleaded and begged for mercy, as the hungry eyes locked onto her.

"No, stay away! Leave me alone! Someone, help me!" she shrieked.

The people in the street ignored her and went on with their business, averting their eyes. Some kids gathered around to cheer and throw rocks at the woman. Jack and his circle of friends, decided to enjoy the nostalgia of watching the wolves at work, like they did when they were kids. A few other students joined them, including the broad shouldered young man.

The woman's time was up. The wolves were done playing with her. Now, the feast could begin. A young hunter swiftly pounced and sank his teeth into the woman's ankle, tugging on her rickety old leg. She shrieked and cried for help. The tearing of aged skin and breaking of brittle bone caused a crowd to gather and watch the spectacle in awe. Some gasped. Some laughed. Most just saw it as what it was: the natural order of things. The woman wailed once more, begging to be saved. A female readied her jaws for the kill.

Then, it happened. Jack couldn't believe his own eyes. The young man with the broad shoulders began beating the wolves off the woman, armed with a pipe. The yelps of pain from the wolves were bone-chilling to the gathered crowd. One unfortunate she-wolf broke her tooth on the pipe, yipping in agony as she slinked away. Unaccustomed to such an attack, the pack fled into the shadows, but did not retreat fully just yet. They had been wronged. Angry howls came from the darkness. A promise had been broken. Their prey had been stolen from them. The howls echoed throughout the city. Sirens soon followed, responding to the cries. Jack preferred the deep howls over the screeching blaring that came with the coming approach of a different kind of predator.

The lawmen arrived at the scene in their large black vans, the vinyl red wolf snarling at the crowd from the vehicle's side. Their sirens blared. Their boots stomped on the hard pavement as they exited, creating a wall of black leather and silver chains between the crowd. With their arms locked together, they stepped forward, pushing Jack and the rest of the spectators back. Not one of them spoke. But their clawed gauntlets and blood-red nightsticks sent a clear message. No-one was to interfere with what would happen next.

The investigator, a corporal with a ranking of two red stars, walked onto the scene. He asked no questions. One look at the woman, the youth and the pipe in his hand, covered in blood and clumps of wolf hair said more than any words could. The corporal walked up to the young man, stopping a few inches short from pressing his black, faceless visor against the youth's face.

"Explain!" he snarled.

"She was hurting," the youth mumbled. "I couldn't . . . I mean, I had—"

The corporal drew his gun and shot the young man twice, a bullet in each knee. He wailed like a child as he fell to the ground. For extra measure, the corporal shot the old woman in her knee as well. Some in the crowd gasped, but the lawman's growls silenced any voices of protest and disgust. The corporal raised his visor slightly and blew his whistle twice, giving the all clear. As suddenly as the lawmen had appeared, they rushed back into their vehicle and sped off into the night, leaving two crippled bags of meat and a crowd too frightened to speak a single word.

Slowly but surely, the crowd began to disperse. A few children lingered to throw stuff at the two doomed souls, but their parents pulled them away, knowing that one bad throw could make them prey as well. It wouldn't be long now. Jack could already see the eyes glinting in the darkness. The hungry growls that grew louder and louder, as soft paws hit the pavement, their claws ticking against concrete.

His friends pulled them away, claiming boredom as their excuse for their exit. Jack looked back once, before walking off with them and trying his best to forget what he'd witnessed. Behind him, he could hear screams and the sound of flesh being torn.

From all around, peeking from every window, nook and cranny, the laughter of children echoed, cheering as the pack dug into their game. But Jack could witness no more. For once, Jack didn't feel like watching the carnage. Something had vanished that day, and the hunt was no longer the spectacle it once was.

The last time Jack ever heard someone speak of the young man was when his face came up during a government bulletin. Apparently, before his violent and unprovoked attack on the pack, the young man had been diagnosed as a violent schizophrenic sexual deviant, guilty of launching into numerous other attacks against wolves throughout the city. It was only now that he had acted in front of witnesses, finally paying for his crimes. Upon searching his home, the lawmen also found a plenitude of evidence that he was pederast as well. In the end, the young man paid the price, and all was well in the world once again. His name was Jack as well.

It was strange, though. While they'd only met on a few occasions, Jack didn't recall the other Jack ever exhibiting any odd behavior of the like. He seemed like a perfectly ordinary young man, if a bit quiet and reserved, but intelligent and compassionate. He couldn't believe that the same young man could be guilty of the crimes associated with him. But it had to be true, didn't it? The bulletin couldn't possibly be wrong. The kid was obviously a sicko. A degenerate who tried to go against the natural order of things. He deserved being torn apart and having his intestines spill into the streets.

At least, that's what Jack told himself every night for the following weeks, just so he could sleep somewhat soundly each night. He tried to forget the other Jack, knowing full well he never would.

As a man of thirty-five, Jack heard. He heard it clearly, even as the familiar voice on the other end of the phone kept pausing to catch her breath. It was his mother, calling him very late in the night. She was hysterical.

"Ma? What is it? What's wrong?"

"Jack . . . your father . . . he hasn't come home. I don't know where he is, Jack. I don't know where he is!"

It had finally come. The call he'd been dreading these past few years, as his parents grew frailer and weaker. Like a fool, his father had gone out for groceries by himself and hadn't come home. It was long past sundown, and the temperatures had dropped fiercely. With the night and the coming winter and regular game being scarce, his father practically served himself to the wolves on a platter.

Jack's mother had asked around the neighborhood, but no-one paid her any mind. His brother didn't answer any of her calls, and the neighbors were ignoring her constant badgering at their door. So mad with fear and hysteria, she was ready to go to town hall and inquire about her missing husband.

"No! You stay where you are," Jack snapped. Having her walk the streets was dangerous enough. But a woman of her age going to town hall and asking the questions no-one wants to answer could have bought her a one-way ticket to a personal session with the lawmen. What was left of her would just be fed to the wolves. He offered to ask around, pleading with his mother to stay indoors and make no attempt to contact the lawmen.

Of course, Jack didn't do as he promised. Yes, he could have asked around about the whereabouts of his father, but what would they tell him he didn't already know? Instead, he drove around all night, trying to come to terms with the truth. They got him. The goddamn wolves got him. His father must have been too slow or careless. *How could he have been so stupid?* Jack knew this day would come sooner or later. With his father's bad knee, worsened eyesight and poor hip, it was a long time coming, inevitable really. But why did it have to be so soon? Why now? Why?

Those damned wolves. Savage beasts. Monsters. Man-eaters. He remembered his childhood, watching the hunters from his window.

It had all seemed funnier back then. Watching someone else's loved ones being run down in the street only to be ripped to shreds. Now it was a terrifying reality for him. *How could Dad have been so foolish to go out alone?* he thought. *Why didn't he ask me to come with him?* But then, what could he have done to help? Surely he couldn't fight the wolves. Or the lawmen. They'd both be chow. *Damned wolves.*

Hours had passed before Jack finally dared to go to his parents' house. He imagined the state his mother would be in. Sobbing and weeping on her couch, hysterical about what was to become of her. It would be up to him to calm her down. With his father gone, all they could do was silently mourn him, then forget he ever existed and move on with their lives. Mentioning him would be a surefire path to more trouble.

Jack parked a block away from his parent's house. While he knew he probably shouldn't have, he felt like walking. Looking around his old street, he couldn't help but feel it wasn't the same place anymore. Had it always been this cold? Did he always feel the hairs on his neck stand up whenever he walked past a darkened alley? He couldn't remember feeling like this before; the feeling of being watched from the darkness, as hungry tongues licked saliva over bared teeth. The street where he grew up changed, without even a single brick being moved.

Then, in the distance, Jack heard a howl. He didn't think much of it at first. It was the chuckles and happy shrieks that roused him out of his funk. The sound of children's laughter.

Then it hit him. *She wouldn't have, would she?* He raced home as quickly as he could, being met with a wide-open door. A woman's slipper lay in the front yard. He ran through the house, checking the kitchen, every room, and even the basement. Nothing. Not a trace of her. He raced outside, looking across the empty street for a sign of her.

"Mom?" he shouted. No answer came, barring the distant howl of the pack.

As a man of forty-eight, Jack trembled. He shook like the last dead leaf fluttering on the end of a branch, pulled by the wind as it desperately tries to hold on. The night he feared for so long had come. The night when he first came face-to-face with death.

After a long day of work at the Office of Property Assessment, he'd taken a short cut into the street with the deli. The Party had imposed a temporary lift on the cigarette ban, so Jack figured he'd stock up on enough smokes to last himself for a while. With three large cartons of cigarettes under his arms, he rushed home. It was then that someone smashed into Jack, throwing them both onto the street. Cigarettes flew in the air before hitting the dirty road. Time slowed down for just a moment, right before Jack violently collided with the cobblestone ground.

For a second, Jack struggled to regain his senses. He felt crushed cigarettes beneath his fingers, dried tobacco sticking to his palms. A man, about ten years his senior, laid on top of him, frantically trying to get up. Jack pushed the man off of him. His arm hurt. Blood seeped into the fabric of his coat. He prayed it wasn't broken. Walking home with a wound would be akin to slathering himself with gravy and serving himself to the hunters on a platter.

"I'm sorry," the older man gasped. "I didn't—"

"Can't you see where you're—" Jack began. A deep baritone snarl interrupted him, freezing both men in place.

A growl. Spittle ran down a set of white daggers that were the wolf's teeth. Jack met the eyes of a lone wolf. Exiled from its pack, starved and desperate for food, it approached the two sacks of meat. The beast was in luck. After chasing the older man for a few blocks, it now had two meals to choose from.

Hungry eyes darted between the two men, gasping their quick and frightened breaths, unsure of which of the two to pick. Its nose twitched, smelling blood in the air. To Jack's horror, the wolf locked its eyes on him. Wounded prey is easier prey, is it not?

"No! Him. I'm not there yet," Jack shouted, frantically pointing at the other man. "Take him! You were after him!"

The predator didn't take to his protests. It was hungry, and food was on the table. What difference does one juicy slab of meat to another make anyway? A good meal as any, even with Jack's slight age difference.

Jack panicked. He needed a weapon. Something to fight the beast off. He felt around, fishing through the sea of cigarettes for anything that he could use to fight back. There! A loose brick in the road. He frantically pried it loose, breaking his nails, blood seeping from his fingertips. He held the brick up high, armed and ready to defend himself. But what difference would it make? Slay the wolf, and the lawmen would serve him up to a different pack. Do nothing, and be eaten. He was trapped.

Then, as suddenly as he appeared, the man who collided with Jack leaped up and rushed away. The wolf's attention snapped back to his original prey. In that instant, Jack jumped up and threw the brick at the fleeing man. A direct hit! The older man fell down and hit the ground. A stream of blood gushed from the back of his head, enough to stir the wolf on.

The predator rushed at the hunk of fresh meat laying in the street, dragging its prey by the leg into an alley. The man screamed and wailed, begging for help. From a window, three children laughed, clapping and cheering for the wolf.

But Jack couldn't laugh. While relieved to be alive, at what cost did he achieve it? He nearly attacked a wolf! He cracked a man's head open with a brick to save his own hide. He stumbled behind a trash can and vomited. Did surviving always feel this wretched?

As the older man's death throes died down, Jack wobbled his way back home. He cursed the loss of his smokes and the pain in his arm. Two lawmen stomped right past him. Jack saw his reflection in their visors and noticed them clenching their tight grip on their night sticks. Younger men, hungry for blood and aching for an excuse to hurt another. While he could not see them, he imagined their eyes, indistinguishable from those of the hunters of the night. For a moment, he couldn't remember which one was the bloody predator that hunted these parasites of society and fed on their meat.

Jack slinked away, afraid of being thrown before those bloody fangs for the second time in one night. His heart raced. He remembered the laughter and the fun it had been, watching the hunt when he was a boy. Did the world change, or was it just him? Had it always been this cold and unforgiving? Was it getting worse each day? In the distance, Jack heard the howls.

At sixty-one, Jack ran.

His time had come. Like so many before him, he had no option left but to run. He ran as fast as he could, though he knew it would never be fast enough.

With every step, his aching joints screamed at him. His heart pumped blood at a tremendous speed, yet he felt like he might as well have been crawling at a snail's pace. The sweat from his brow stung his eyes. Breathing became a nightmare, as he hacked up dark blotches of phlegm with each exhale.

There were two others that ran as well, a woman and a man. They were behind him a minute ago, but the pack got one of them. Jack had no idea which one, nor did he care anymore. Where the second one went, he didn't know either.

High pitched cheering came from above. The neighborhood children laughed at him, as they watched the spectacle of the old man frantically stumbling down the empty street, possessed by some mad hope of escape. Jack tried to not let it get to him. If it wasn't for the hunters chasing him, he'd have stopped to scream at them.

Curse their little cold hearts. Cruel little beasts, he thought, remembering his own cheers and laughter very well.

If you asked him now, he couldn't tell you why he ever thought the hunt had been funny. *Why? Why are you laughing? I'm being hunted down like some dirty rodent! Like filth. But I'm not filth. I'm a man! Why is this happening to me?* He could cry for help, but what would be the point? He never helped anyone in all those years when he watched the hunt. Why would anyone do the same for him?

The yipping and growling grew closer. No time to vent his rage, being so close to home now, with still a chance that he could make it. With any luck, there wouldn't be any lawmen loitering in front of his building, allowing him to slip inside and hide from the pack. If there were, they might just sweep his legs out from under him and throw him back to the wolves. No, he had to risk it. It was his only chance.

There it was! The steps to his building. Home! Safe! And not a lawman in sight. He could make it. He would make it!

Then, it happened. An agonizing pain in his wrist that dragged Jack to the ground. He fought, trying to pull his arm out from the sleeve of his jacket, but the young wolf had his teeth buried deep into his flesh. It burned! The pain burned so much!

A second pain, from his thigh. A third on his ankle. The rest of the pack joined in, prancing and jumping around Jack as the three pulled him to the ground. His head hit the pavement, gushing blood out from the wound. They won.

He turned around, flailing his arms. An immense pressure pushed down on his chest. Was his heart giving out? No, it was one of them. A beautiful she-wolf with bright gray fur and azure eyes loomed over him. Her teeth bared as she snapped at her pack. The others backed off. This was *her* kill.

Jack looked into her eyes, seeing himself reflected in those spheres. Big caerulean marbles, showing him an image of what he had become. He saw an old man. An old man like so many before him. Beyond his reflection, was darkness. A cold empty void, yet one that was very much alive, burning with a primal fire of passion. It was her. The she-wolf. She looked back into his very soul, as if to thank him for being her kill. It was his time.

The laughter stopped. Or perhaps he just didn't hear it. There was nothing left but silence. For a moment, it was like there was only them. Just Jack and the she-wolf.

"Beautiful," he whispered.

Then her teeth sank into his face. Warm breath stroked his skin as her canines scraped against bone. The pain began after she pulled away, taking most of his face along with it. Another bite! He tried to scream, but he no longer had a throat. He heard the laughter again, as another wolf sank its teeth into his crotch. Young voices, laughing as the old man was torn apart by the beautiful hunters of the night.

Joachim Heijndermans is a writer and artist from the Netherlands. His work has been featured in Gathering Storm, Mad Scientist Journal, Kraxon, Storyteller, Every Day Fiction and Asymmetry Fiction, with upcoming publications with Ares Magazine, Metaphorosis and the anthology *Enter the Aftermath*. He likes to read, travel and collect toys, and is currently completing his first children's book.

LUMP

By D.J. Tyrer

"That looks nasty," I said, peering at Alan's back. He was sitting on the edge of my bath, where the light was best, and had taken his shirt off to offer me a look. Amongst the pimples that clustered upon his back, there was a large lump like a red, inflamed Satsuma. "Does it hurt?"

He shrugged. "Not really. It's uncomfortable, not sore."

"What caused it? Do you know?" It looked like an allergic reaction, but seemed too localised.

Alan pulled his shirt back on, then turned to face me. "That's the strange thing."

"Why?"

"It happened to me in a dream," he said, and he began to tell me what had happened.

Alan was walking through the dark, misty streets of an unfamiliar city. His footsteps echoed hollowly about him. He could see nobody else, but he could hear the occasional echo of a horse's hooves, a distant inarticulate shout or a muffled scream.

Although he had no conscious idea of where he was going, he kept walking despite the fear he felt building at the strange sounds echoing off the cyclopean walls that surrounded him. Somehow, he knew that stopping would place him in danger. What danger . . . he couldn't say.

Then, he came to his destination. He didn't know how he knew it, but the ironbound door in the alley wall of some old and soaring building was where he was meant to be. He reached out and tried the cold, wrought-iron handle: it was unlocked. The door swung open to reveal a void within.

Biting his lip for a minute, Alan resolved to press on. He stepped into the darkness and, a few steps later, stumbled out into a courtyard reminiscent of Moorish Spain, lit by the light of the moons above. There were no plants, only urns he didn't dare look into, and the pool at the courtyard's centre was dry and its fountain long dead.

Alan stood for a moment, savouring the silence, and wondering why he was there.

Then, he became aware of a new and unnerving sound, something like the swishing of skirts or the rustle of leaves. He looked about for the source of the noise, but could see nothing in the darkness beyond the arches at the courtyard's edge.

He called out, but there was no reply, only the *swish-swish*.

Alan wanted to run, but didn't know where. Then, *it* came into view. From the shadows, something flopped and slithered its way into the courtyard and towards him. It looked like a bundle of washed-out yellow rags from under which, for just a moment, a tiny, porcelain-white limb, like that of a baby, would protrude, then disappear back within the folds.

Alan looked down at it and one end of it rose as if to look up at him in return. They stayed like that for a long moment. Alan wasn't certain whether to feel fear or be amused. Had it been made of brightly-coloured cloth, he might have found it almost cute: it gave the impression of a little pet seeking love. Yet, it very clearly wasn't natural and it disturbed him.

Then, it suddenly rolled sideways. He turned to follow it, but a moment later, it was behind him and he felt a dozen tiny hands clutching at his legs, pulling the thing up his trousers and, then, his jacket. He tried to grab for it, but somehow he couldn't reach it.

There was a ripping sound as his shirt tore and he felt a piercing sensation, as if he'd been bitten on his back.

"Then, I woke up with a scream. Of course, although I could feel the pain, I thought it was just the echo of a dream. I didn't think it was anything more, just went back to sleep."

"And, then you got the lump?"

Alan nodded. "Yes. It was there the next morning. It was only small. As time passed, it got bigger, but hurt less."

"Strange. You should see a doctor."

He shrugged. "Maybe."

He didn't, of course. Alan was never the sort to trust a professional. He might ask a friend, but usually he'd do it himself, or do nothing at all. When his pipes had burst, he'd tolerated a puddle in his lounge for a fortnight before finally calling a plumber.

"It's gotten larger," he said when next I saw him.

It had. It was now the size of a football and he could've auditioned to play Richard III.

"You really should see a doctor," I said, staring at the livid, red mass.

"I don't like to make a fuss. I mean, it doesn't hurt."

"Are you sure?" It had to.

"No, not really. It's just uncomfortable; heavy."

"You don't say . . ."

It looked horrible, like some sort of cyst or tumour. It was one of those things that fascinates you and repels you in equal measure; I had the urge to touch it, but, at the same time, didn't want to. It made me feel queasy.

"Hell!" I suddenly cried, jumping back from him.

"What?" exclaimed Alan, turning his head to look at me. "What is it?"

I didn't answer. I couldn't believe it. I leaned forward to look at the lump, certain I'd been wrong.

I hadn't. I gasped.

"What is it?" Alan whined, worried.

"Um . . . I don't know how to . . ."

"What? Tell me!"

I watched as, yet again, a face pressed itself against the inside of his skin and the shape of a tiny fist pushed out the surface of the lump. Surely, I was seeing things! And, yet, there it was . . .

"Alan . . . I think there's a baby in your bump . . ."

"I dreamed of a child," he murmured, taking it more calmly than I did.

Alan had been in a suite of rooms, which he didn't recognise, yet somehow knew to be his home. He was, apparently, high up within some sort of tower: there was a balcony from which he had a view of an endless city of soaring towers rising from a sea of mist. It was the city from his previous dream.

He walked through the rooms, which had an air of decayed gentility about them, until he came to one with vibrantly-yellow walls and a cot.

In the cot, there was a child. He could hear it snuffling. Slowly, tentatively, he walked towards it. He felt an odd sense of nerves.

"Then, I woke," he finished. "I never did see the baby. I don't know what it meant. Well, not till now . . ."

"You need to go see a doctor. You need to be checked out."

"And be poked and prodded? No, thank you!"

It was a month later that he called me in a panic and asked me to come over. He hadn't been out in all that time, had hidden away, ashamed, fearful.

I rushed round and let myself in with the key he kept under a flowerpot beside his backdoor as an invitation to burglars.

"Alan, you there?"

An agonised groan guided me to his front room.

Alan was on the floor in his underpants. The bulge had grown to enormous proportions and the skin was stretched horribly thin and appeared to be beginning to split. Within it, I could clearly see the . . . baby twisting about, extending its arms and legs to pull the skin taut: trying to break free.

"It hurts!" he cried, writhing on the floor. "It hurts so much! Do something!"

I didn't know what to do. If I phoned for an ambulance, what could I tell them?

I just stared in horrified fascination.

Then, the skin burst and it broke free in a shower of puss-blotched blood. Bile rose in my throat.

It wasn't a baby. Not a human one, anyway.

It was the general size and shape of a baby and the yellow of its skin might have been attributable to jaundice, but the hollows where the eyes should've been were covered with skin and its eyes were in the palms of its hands, which it held up to observe me.

The *thing* slithered down Alan's back and flopped onto the bloodstained carpet. Then, it half-crawled and half-flopped towards the corner of the room and pulled itself up into a sitting position, leaving Alan sobbing in the centre of the room. I stood transfixed, unable to act.

The creature began to croon, a strange, phlegm-filled tune that reminded me of *Beautiful Dreamer*. As I watched, a shimmer appeared in the air. The shimmer seemed to coalesce into a circle that looked like a mirror floating in the air; only its greyish surface reflected nothing. Then, it seemed to wobble, a little like a pond into which a stone has dropped and an image began to form of a dark and barren landscape.

It crawled through the opening between this world and that one and I watched it crawl some distance across that barren landscape, before pulling itself once more into a sitting position.

Then, it began to croon again, a different song this time, one I couldn't place at all. Dust began to swirl about it and, as I watched, the ground trembled and lances of rock began to extrude upwards from the earth, growing into towers that reached towards the moons that began to accrete from the whirling clouds of sand. The creature—the child, or whatever it was, that had sprung Minerva-like from my friend's back—appeared to be singing a new world into existence. A world over which that peculiar yellow thing would be king. A world that showed a certain affinity to the one Alan had seen in his dreams. Coincidence? I didn't think so. Had those dreams been a pre-echo of what it was now creating here? Or, was the entity somehow self-created?

Either way, I was fascinated, the amazing sight of creation sweeping aside the nausea I'd felt watching its birth. I felt the urge to step through the gateway and join it in that new world, explore it, experience it—live it. But, at the same time, I knew such a step would be irreversible. If I went there, I'd never return; I'd be leaving everything behind.

A new world!

My courage failed me and I looked away. I so wanted to leave, yet couldn't bring myself to abandon my banal life: I'd invested so much in it . . .

When I looked back, the gateway was gone, that window to another world was closed: my chance at a new life in a new world of unknown delights and new experiences was gone. It was over.

Alan groaned and I crouched beside him.

I should've stepped through.

DJ Tyrer is the person behind *Atlantean Publishing* and has been widely published in anthologies and magazines around the world, such as *Chilling Horror Short Stories* (Flame Tree), *Snowpocalypse* (Black Mirror Press), *Steampunk Cthulhu* (Chaosium), *Night in New Orleans* (FunDead Publications), *Miskatonic Dreams* (Alban

Lake), and *Sorcery & Sanctity: A Homage to Arthur Machen* (Hieroglyphics Press), and in addition, has a novella available in paperback and on the Kindle, *The Yellow House* (Dunhams Manor).

BONJOUR, STEVIE

By David Turton

From: Cliff and Mary Allan <cliffandmary-allan1951@gmail.com>
Date: Sat, 9 Sep 2017 at 2:48 PM
Subject: Hello from France
To: Stephanie Allen <steviejanineallen451@out-look.com>

Bonjour, Stevie!

I'll be honest, that's pretty much exhausted my French repertoire. Your mother, brother and I arrived a few days ago. We are enjoying the hustle and bustle of Paris after the inevitable trauma of the long-haul flight to get here. We were in premium economy, which is the most minute of smidgens above economy class, and found ourselves sitting behind a young couple with a delightful baby. I had knocked back as much Valium as I possibly could in order to get some sleep. As you know, I abhor even the shortest of flights and suffer from the most terrible anxiety on those large iron death traps, whereas your mother could sleep through a Slipknot concert. So, just as the drug was beginning to take its effect, the sly little baby started bawling. "*Waaah, waaah, waaah,*" it yelled, each scream louder and more piercing than the last. As a father of two, including yourself, Stevie, I know what it's like to have a baby crying uncontrollably. But that doesn't mean that I have to tolerate it in my senior years. It sounded like each yell was stabbing coldly into my soul, and you know no-one wants to find out what's in there. Anyway, the baby's cries were dealt with, but they were soon replaced with its mother's screams. That's life I suppose, you remove one problem and just replace it with one that is just as troublesome.

Anyway, enough of that.

We are staying in the Marais district of Paris. I have to say, Stevie, it's very trendy. We are by far the oldest people around, apart from Mikey of course. Speaking of your little brother, he has been quiet since we set off. Of course, we haven't told him about the true purpose of this trip, but I feel that he suspects it on some level. We toyed with the idea of letting him know, just so he could make the most of his last few days, especially in so wonderful a city as Paris, but we couldn't be certain that he wouldn't cause problems with our carefully planned trip. I'm sure that, if he can, he'll look back at his part in our pilgrimage with pride. It's a nice thought for me and your mother.

We did a walking tour of the Marais on a stinking hot day, one of those times when the sweat just seems to soak every inch of your clothing. I'm not quite as fit as I used to be, but I kept up with your mother and Mikey admirably if I do say so myself. I visited the Louvre for the first time and was overwhelmed by the vastness of its collections. It was really awesome, Stevie, I only wish you could be here to enjoy it with us. I'm sure you're lying on the sofa as you read this, stroking your baby bump and picturing all the masterpieces on display. Seriously, I was overwhelmed and I'm not so manly to deny that I shed a tear when I saw Gericault's *The Raft of the Medusa*. Such darkness, such life brought to a macabre and deathly story. Your mother and Mikey weren't really passionate about our Louvre trip, and I lamented your absence more then than ever, you know how much I adore our shared love of art. You may never come to Paris, Stevie, but I hope to show it to you in the next life, if the Great Old Ones see fit to allow it.

Talking of passions, the food here is amazing. It certainly is not an exaggeration or a myth about the French cuisine. It really is exquisite, Stevie. Although I'm not sure I impressed the waitress and the other diners in one of the classier Marais restaurants. I wanted a steak and, as the waitress had little English, I did my best cow impression, placing my fingers on my head to act as horns and creating an impressively accurate *mooooooo* sound. The waitress laughed, more out of politeness than anything else, and your mother was mortified. When the food came, I was given pork. Whoever thought it was a good idea to allow Americans passports, eh?

In the afternoon, we took a bicycle trip along the Loire River to Amboise, one you would have really enjoyed, Stevie. The countryside is unbelievable, the whole Loire valley is just sublime. In another life, I could see ourselves living there, drinking crisp chardonnay and eating cheese and olives.

Back in the city and everything went to plan in the catacombs. How wonderful they were, all the bones stacked up like death himself had laid the foundations for the city. Isn't it wonderfully poetic, Stevie, that one of the happiest, love-filled cities on our planet is built on an underlayer of death and decay? What a lovely metaphor for life, that it owes its very existence to the strength of death and darkness below. We were overwhelmed and this time, your mother shared my passion and joy. You would have too, Stevie, oh if only you could have seen it, especially someone as educated as you. In fact, our tour guide had a similar background to yourself, with his first degree in history and a master's degree in archaeology. I enjoyed chatting to him so much I nearly let slip about our journey back in February to the Valley of Hinnom, and our discovery of some of the original pages of the *Necronomicom.* Of course, I'm not sure how he would have taken that story, and I didn't want to draw any unwanted attention to us, but he was a wonderfully insightful and interesting man. I almost felt guilty slipping the keys from his pocket, but as you know, Stevie, the plan comes first.

Finally, your mother and I have been enjoying French food and wine somewhat to excess. In order to work off the calories we have been walking a lot. I have had on that pedometer you gave me the whole time and have clocked up 40ks so far. Not bad for an old man, eh?

We are just getting ready now to go back to the catacombs and execute the plan. I keep looking at Mikey and thinking of when he was a baby, a decade ago. It fills your mother and I with sadness, and I'm sure it does you too, that this will be his final night but I suppose if all goes to plan, we could say that about all of us before too long. Hell, you could say that about that all of us anyway if you fast forward a few years, even the little foetus growing inside you as we speak. Death is something to be embraced, not feared. Why fear something that comes to each and every one of us, the great leveller? But I suppose one of our flaws as humans is that we have these childish emotions that we can't simply cast off the way we would discard bad habits. As I type, I'm looking at the dagger we excavated from the cave in Hinnom. How beautiful it is, with the metal tentacles wrapping around the handle, and it's just so wonderfully old. I'm so glad we managed to sneak it through customs. I just hope that those pages of the *Necronomicon* are right, or that we translated them correctly. I guess we'll know soon enough, and I'll email you as soon as I have any updates.

Hope you and bump are happy and healthy.

Love from Dad, Mom, and Mikey

PS The international dongle thing you sorted out for me works a treat. I just put it in my laptop and boom—it connects to the internet. What a wonderful invention!

From: Cliff and Mary Allan <cliffandmary-allan1951@gmail.com>
Date: Mon, 11 Sep 2017 at 09:18 PM
Subject: An update from France!
To: Stephanie Allen <steviejanineallen451@out-look.com>

Bonjour again, Stevie! Comment est la vie?

See, I'm picking it up more and more! By the end of this trip, I'll be able to pass for a bona fide Frenchman myself. Well, okay, maybe not but I'm certainly improving.

All went to plan in the catacombs and your brother is no longer with us. It went like clockwork, so thanks for all your help in preparing our approach to this.

We held hands after we used the dagger on him, I'm not ashamed to admit that we both cried and hugged as his eyes disappeared into whites and blood spewed from the slit I'd made in his neck. But seeing the crimson blood glisten on the dagger was truly a remarkable experience, magical even. And his blood sprayed all over the bones as per our plan, which was magnificent to watch. I'm sure you'll be sad at little Mikey passing on, but at least we know we are doing it for a truly great cause. Of course, we read the passage from the book's pages. It was amazing to read words that Abdul Alhazred himself had written all those centuries ago, as the blood dripped from those old skeletons below the streets of Paris. Maybe part of Mikey will live on in your child. I really do believe that, Stevie, as his life ended with the words from the *Necronomicon*, just as your baby was conceived with a similar ritual. Maybe we will have Mikey version two with us before long.

Has it worked? We don't know yet. We'll stick around in Paris for a few more days and, if nothing occurs, we'll head back to California to see you. Don't get me wrong, it will be brilliant to see you again, but it will be disappointing if nothing happens. And the longer time goes on, the more your mother and I feel despondent that something hasn't gone right. But at least we've had a brilliant holiday on the back of it and we will definitely bring you here one day if that is the case. As I said in my previous email, you will absolutely adore the Louvre, not to mention the food and wine. So, if the worst-case scenario is that we did something wrong, or that the Great Old Ones remain asleep, I'm sure we'll make the best of it. My only semblance of optimism about the whole thing is that the dreams we've been having are even more vivid and terrifying than before. Do your dreams still haunt you in the same way? It's quite thrilling isn't it, Stevie, to wake in your own cold sweat, covered in goosebumps? An exhilaration like no other, that's what your mother and I feel.

Oh, I nearly forgot, we went up the Eiffel Tower today! Can you believe that? It's a strange thing, full of beauty at the same time as being an industrial structure, a mass of dark grey metal and ominous shapes. I feel that it has no place amongst the stunning Paris architecture, but then I suppose it's almost like it could have burst out from the darkness below the city's streets. And I kind of like that thought. The views from the top were sublime, it was a bright, clear day and we could see for miles.

Sorry for the brevity of this email, we're about to go for another meal. I swear I've put ten pounds on in little more than a week. If we do come back in a few days, I may have to pay for an extra seat on the airlines!

Best wishes to you and bump, and aurevoir for now,

Mom and Dad

From: Cliff and Mary Allan <cliffandmary-allan1951@gmail.com>
Date: Tue 12 Sep 2017 at 11:28 PM
Subject: It worked!
To: Stephanie Allen <steviejanineallen451@out-look.com>

Stevie,

I'm typing this quickly and excitedly, so please excuse any typos, I know you're a bit of a pedant when it comes to the use of English!

What can I say other than—IT WORKED! We were having a beautiful meal in the Montmarte district of the city, on a mezzanine balcony overlooking a busy street, and we heard a rumbling from below us. Obviously, living in Cali, we assumed we had a minor quake coming and barely batted an eyelid. But this is France, Stevie, they hardly have anything like that over here. People were panicking and running, thinking there was some natural disaster, but we stayed still, holding hands.

That's when we saw them. They were covered in black wispy smoke, but we knew straight away what they were. They were the bones, Stevie! The bones from below, from those wonderful catacombs, had pushed themselves to the surface of the city. As they walked, everyone in front of them fell down and just rotted. Like they were decomposing in front of our eyes. We saw two, then three, then four. And the most amazing thing? The people that fell and rotted rose from the ground and began walking once more, their eyes a glazed red. They walked straight past me and your mother. Maybe we just weren't in their path, they seemed to be sticking to the main street below us. Or maybe we were protected by our part in their awakening. Either way, we smiled at each other like lovesick teenagers, paid the bill and walked back to the hotel, where I'm now emailing you from.

We've been looking out of our hotel window, and it looks like chaos has taken over the city. Pockets of fire are breaking out all over the place and we can hear absolute and total panic. It's gripped this city like a fast-moving plague and we can smell the fear rising up from the streets. The river has burst its banks and huge pools of water have appeared all over the city below us. The dead march and march and their numbers continue to grow with each person that falls before them, before reanimating. I can see them all below us now, the hordes of undead killers.

You would love the chaos here, Stevie. And most of all, it means that Mikey died for good reason. It was him that let these fantastic beings out. I'm sure you'll be watching it on the news and smiling. Our plan worked so well and a lot of that is down to you. I can see hordes of these beings below us now, they are marching almost robotically. The dark mist follows them and Paris itself has been cast in darkness, even though it is only mid-morning. The blackness rises from deep below the catacombs and I feel only true excitement to see what we may have awoken from below.

I'll update you when I can, Stevie, but I'm sure you agree the monumental achievement this represents for us all. I am confident that we will have a special place in the new world.

I must go now, we are heading back down, we may even meet one of the Great Old Ones, if they have appeared amongst the army of the dead that have risen in their name.

Love to you and bump. If we don't see each other again in this life, we'll catch up with coffee and cake in the next.

Mom and Dad xxx

From: Cliff and Mary Allan <cliffandmary-allan1951@gmail.com>
Date: Tue 12 Sep at 15:40 PM
Subject: Urgent
To: Stephanie Allen <steviejanineallen451@out-look.com>

Stevie, this is going to be brief. Unfortunately, we lost your mother. We were a little over confident and walked into the path of one of the walking stacks of bones. She fell and rotted in their path like the rest of them. I saw her, Stevie, disintegrating in front of my eyes. Again, those childish emotions overruled my logical thoughts and I ran back to the hotel, buried my head in the pillow and wept. How feeble I must be in the eyes of the Great Old Ones. How I only hope they can forgive me and we can all be reunited in the next world.

I have no doubt that this will be my last email, Stevie. The internet connection is intermittent at best and I can't see any flights leaving Paris in the near future. You wouldn't believe the scenes outside the hotel. Darkness has just engulfed the city. I'm sure you're watching the coverage. I had a quick look myself, to see what the outside world made of these events and I see there are the typical claims of terrorism, rioting, natural disasters and the like. I did see one article that gave me immense hope though, Stevie. Hope that the baby growing inside you is destined for greatness. There is a tsunami coming your way, due to hit the West Coast in the next few hours. A massive, unspeakable being is rising from the depths of the Pacific, its tentacles are said to be reaching high out of the water. He is coming for his unborn son, Stevie. Be ready for him. We are ready to join the Great Cthulhu in the new world. I love you more than you know and I will see you in the next life.

Hail Great Cthulhu. Hail his prince. Hail the new world.

See you around. Au revoir mon amour.

Dad X

David Turton has extensive training in Journalism, Marketing and Public Relations and has been writing as a career for over fourteen years. A huge horror fiction fan, particularly the works of Stephen King, David has written several short stories, all centred around dark tales of horror and dystopia. He is also in the final stages of his first novel, an apocalyptic horror set in the near future.

Follow David on Twitter @davidturton and visit David's new website!

DEMONS (2017) and the Quest of Indie Film

A Gehenna Post Review

(Originally published on the Gehenna Post)

Greetings from the Ether,

We were given the honor to attend an early screening of Demons, a new horror film from Mississippi powerhouse Miles Doleac (American Horror Story, The Magnificent Seven). We would first like to thank the director for the invite and for him reaching out to the Gehenna Post. We hope this will be the first of many, many more early reviews.

Alas, let's begin!

Former priest Colin Hampstead turns to a career as an author after an attempted exorcism goes wrong. The victim of said possession is none other than the younger sister of the woman he later marries. Together, and many years after the tragic incident, they battle the demons that aim to put them down, coming to realizations and truths about themselves in the process.

Now, the first thing that must be noted and thoroughly considered, is the fact that this film is not a Hollywood blockbuster. It is not on tier with many Oscar-nominated films. For average moviegoers, the experience may not be what they would hope. Nonetheless, the ability to admire the work that these artists put their hearts and souls into, with the limited resources they had, is something that we should take into acknowledgment.

There are good performances here, most notably from John Schneider (Smallville), Andrew Divoff (Wishmaster), and Steven Brand (The Scorpion King). Unlike previous outings with Doleac as director, he chose (in a risk that truly paid off) to put other cast members to the forefront. The character of Colin (played by Miles Doleac) is well done, as all of the director's onscreen performances have been to date, but he truly gave the floor to other stars in a way that hasn't been seen and this was perhaps one of the most respectable decisions made.

Doleac's previous directorial and starring outings, The Historian and The Hollow were both in the field of drama, one being a cinematic academia-based investigation, and the latter being a southern crime noir. Stepping into the realm of horror was brave, and though Doleac doesn't have the most experience in this genre, his skill as a director and screenwriter shine through. There are some solid scares and a few very intense moments throughout the film, while maintaining a structure that is at times changing pretty fast-paced, but at other times seamless. During the Q&A, we asked the director about the challenges he faced tackling the genre of horror, and he said something that we found to be very truthful, horror is "character-driven." The reveals and expanding plot development surrounding the possession and why it happened are exactly that. This, Doleac nailed on the head.

Keeping in mind the struggles that indie filmmakers face in today's industry, Doleac continues to impress with the resources he is given. In the Q&A after the film, the director revealed that the script was written relatively quickly, and despite the rushed nature of this animal's creation, there is some honest storytelling to be seen. If the director can write a screenplay like this in such a short time, one can only imagine his capabilities if given the proper resources and time.

Demons has flaws, and doesn't quite surpass what The Hollow achieved, but it is still worth watching, and more importantly, worth supporting. In a day and age where independent filmmakers struggle to gain recognition and have to work endlessly and tirelessly to produce a movie, it is more important now than ever to support indie films. As Doleac pointed out in the Q&A, the theater industry is dying and it is near impossible to work from the ground up, setting your own foundations in the process.

Many facets of the film didn't work, but the ones that did made up for it. It will be interesting to see where Doleac goes from here and if he chooses to pursue horror again. We are excited to see his progression as a director, actor, and screenwriter. We encourage you, our readers, to watch this film and to support indie film-making. *Demons* is not The Exorcist or The Conjuring but we hope it is the first in an ever-improving filmography from Miles Doleac.

Stream the film on Amazon.

A photo with Demons director Miles Doleac after the screening.

BLADE RUNNER 2049:
Modern Struggles of a Visual Masterpiece

A Gehenna Post Review

(Originally published on the Gehenna Post)

Greetings from the Ether,

We had announced a review for Blade Runner 2049 a couple days ago, following our review of the original, and after seeing the early showing. Our hesitation was based in the fact that this film needed time to digest. The film was breathtaking, mind-boggling, and possibly one of the most beautiful movies to ever be made. Despite these facets, the scope of 2049 is so vast and encompassing, that a good evaluation could not be made directly after the first viewing. As the film has processed in our brains, we feel we are ready to tackle one of the greatest sequels ever made and a true masterclass artistic piece.

Nevertheless, let's dive into this dystopia!

Following a detective as he investigates the mystery of a missing child, K finds himself in the middle of a conspiracy that may not only change his life forever, but also permanently alter the world around him as well.

Blade Runner 2049 is a masterpiece. Plain and simple. No questions asked, no arguments worth discussing. Is it a flawed masterpiece? Yes. Just as its predecessor had flaws, this sequel also does. These minute flaws do not overshadow the surreal, brooding tale that is this film. Director Denis Villeneuve parallels the talents of Ridley Scott's direction of the original. Stacked floor to ceiling with an all star cast, capturing a gloomy, dystopian universe, and once again tackling questions of morality and the human condition, Blade Runner 2049 is just as poignant and important as the original film was, especially in today's box office climate.

K is brought to life by an outstanding performance from Ryan Gosling. Harrison Ford reprises his role as Rick Deckard and delivers an emotional take that is little seen from the Hollywood legend. Sylvia Hoeks nails her turn as the chillingly brutal replicant Luv. Jared Leto does a great job as Tyrell heir, Wallace. Dave Bautista only continues his ever-improving acting talents as Sapper Morton, Robin Wright also fantastic as Lieutenant Joshi. Ana de Armas is haunting and beautiful as Joi, delivering an integral piece to the film for the protagonist K.

Roger Deakins' cinematography is visually stunning and immaculate in every sense of the word. Denis Villeneuve's direction is meticulous and paced at a speed that only builds tension, throttling audiences into the gruesome finale at the end of a long fuse. Each shot of this film feels planned, exacted to perfection, and even destined in a sense. Not a single moment in the film is short of unbelievable. Long pans of desolate cities, overhead angles of the dark, rainy vision of Los Angeles, each setting thoroughly thought out and passionately executed.

Some moments of the film can drag during the nearly three-hour runtime, though they bear little credence to the overall structure and narrative. A few characters weren't explored enough, though again, it doesn't affect the overall movie. With the long runtime the crew were afforded, they definitely made the most out of every second.

When you see Blade Runner 2049, be prepared for an experience. Not a film. Not a movie. Not pure entertainment. Expect an engaging, philosophical masterwork that delivers all the promises the original held for us. The film is not constant action and explosions, it's not fast-paced. 2049 is a slow building pressure cooker filled with cinematic wonders that explodes with a deafening climax, presenting a chilling twist to finalize an existential journey.

There are many surprises in Blade Runner 2049, so whatever you do, **DO NOT** read any spoiler reviews or watch any online. Go to this film with an open mind and as little knowledge as you can. You will not be disappointed.

As you likely read in the title, we are going to discuss the struggles Blade Runner 2049 has been facing in the box office. Originally projected with a $50M opening, 2049 has barely broken the $35M point by the end of the weekend. Yet IMDB has it nestled in their Top 250 Films of All Time, Rotten Tomatoes has it "certified fresh." Metacritic has an amazing score for it. So why isn't it grossing as much as expected?

There are many answers to this question from many sources. The one we have stuck to the most, is that philosophical and artistic cinema has died in the collective consciousness of general moviegoers. Without heroes in spandex ripping corny one-liners as they defeat a super-villain, or giant robots created purely from CGI battling their equally computer-generated opponents, most films are doomed to fail. Denis Villeneuve has made nothing but fascinating and expertly directed films, yet the opening weekend of 2049 barely beat his previous box office record with his outstanding sci-fi flick, Arrival.

Blade Runner 2049, like its predecessor, is a film that requires thought and sincere questioning. It is not spoon fed to the audience. It is not non-stop action from start to finish. It seems that when movies like *Transformers: The Last Knight* can easily make back their budget, but films like 2049 have to rely on Asia to save them from being a financial disaster, we have reached a peak of short attention spans. Audiences often forget that before Star Wars, not many films had a fast pace. They relied on storytelling and visual techniques to convey interest.

We find it needless to say that cinema is dying for general audiences, and if a film as spectacular and thought-provoking as Blade Runner 2049 can struggle at the box office, there is no more denying the dumbing down of general theatrical audiences. Hopefully, 2049 will reinvigorate moviegoers into appreciating film again for the storytelling and cinematography. But again, much like its predecessor, it seems this film may be considered a flop at the box office, regardless of the quality and sheer scope of the film.

We highly encourage you all to see Blade Runner 2049. Don't watch any form of reviews with spoilers and be prepared mentally to leap into another universe. 2049 is not just one of the greatest sequels ever made, it is also a soon-to-be classic in Science Fiction.

Who ever said lightning didn't strike twice in the same place?

If you enjoyed **Hinnom Magazine**, make sure to leave a review on Amazon and follow us on social media!

Facebook: www.facebook.com/gehennaandhinnom-books
Twitter: www.twitter.com/GehennaBooks
Website: www.gehennaandhinnom.wordpress.com

Look out for our releases in 2017!

June 30th, 2017

Hinnom Magazine Issue 001

August 31st, 2017

Hinnom Magazine Issue 002

September 30th, 2017

Year's Best Body Horror 2017 Anthology

October 31st, 2017

Hinnom Magazine Issue 003

November 30th, 2017

Year's Best Transhuman SF 2017 Anthology

December 31st, 2017

Hinnom Magazine Issue 004